POP GIRL

SIGNED WITH A

TALLIA STORM

AND LUCY COURTENAY

For Tessa and Sascha

Scholastic Children's Books
An imprint of Scholastic Ltd
Euston House, 24 Eversholt Street, London, NW1 1DB, UK
Registered office: Westfield Road, Southam, Warwickshire, CV47 0RA
SCHOLASTIC and associated logos are trademarks and/or
registered trademarks of Scholastic Inc.

First published in the UK by Scholastic Ltd, 2017

Text copyright © Tallia Storm, 2017

The right of Tallia Storm to be identified as the author of this work
has been asserted by her.

ISBN 978 1407 15939 3

A CIP catalogue record for this book is available
from the British Library.

Printed by CPI Group (UK) Ltd, Croydon, CR0 4YY
Papers used by Scholastic Children's Books are made
from wood grown in sustainable forests.

1 3 5 7 9 10 8 6 4 2

The lyrics of "Time" and "Pop Girl" are printed courtesy of HH Music Ltd.
Copyright © 2017. All rights reserved.

CHAPTER 1

I know I'm not supposed to admit it, but being famous is pretty fun.

First, you don't get stupid remarks about being named after a weather phenomenon. Instead of dumb cracks about "go rain somewhere else" and having siblings named Drizzle and Hail, I get actual COMPLIMENTS. Everyone's like, "Wow, Storm's such an epic name!" or "Your parents knew you would be famous the minute they named you Storm!" or – my personal fave – "You're a perfect Storm!" which was particularly cool and on my Twitter feed the other day.

"You always used to complain about it," Belle

reminds me as we sit chowing through two enormous bowls of complimentary ice cream.

Complimentary means FREE. This is the second fun thing about fame. I sometimes get free ice cream in this place because I'm famous and they want people to know that I'm into them, which I totally am. I'm SO up for this whole celebrity lifestyle.

I have an enormous ball of peanut-caramel ice cream (NOMSVILLE) in my mouth and so Belle has to wait until I have dealt with it before I reply.

"Maybe once," I say as all that icy yumminess tingles through my brain. "But I'm not complaining now."

Two girls have stopped outside the window of the ice-cream parlour. They are peering inside, cupping their hands round their eyes to get a better squizz at me. I wave cheerfully, sending a few splodges of ice cream across the table. They explode into giggles and wave back.

This, of course, is fun thing number three. Being recognized.

"Shame about your surname though," Belle says.

Peeling my gaze from my two street-side fans, I eye my best friend as she swirls her double-mint-strawberry-sundae combo into a greeny, pinky whirlpool. She's got an innocent look on her face, which means we are halfway through Operation Wind Up Storm.

"What's wrong with my surname?" I say.

"Hall means corridor. Sorry, but there it is. It's not exactly blingtastic."

"Jerry's done OK with Hall," I return, a bit indignantly.

"You could say the same about Albert," Belle replies.

I frown. "Is he that indie pop guy with the goatee?"

"Think about it, you idiot!"

We both snort a lot about me thinking *the* Albert Hall had a goatee.

"Anyway," I say when I have stopped laughing. "I won't need my surname for much longer. I'm going to be like Rihanna. Who even knows what her surname is?"

"Ambitious much?" Belle says.

"You have to be ambitious to get where you want to go," I tell her, wagging my spoon for extra emphasis. "That's what Ivy told me. She said most people will never understand what it's really like to be a star" – I give Belle a wink – "and that I just had to do what I know is right for me, no matter what it takes. No apologies."

"*This* again." Belle rolls her eyes, but she is smiling as she sucks on her spoon. She pretends not to want to hear about it, but Ivy's all we've been able to talk about for weeks.

"Excuse me, are you Storm Hall?"

It's the two girls from outside. Except they are now inside. I put down my ice-cream spoon and hope I don't have a blob on my nose.

"Yes," I say, beaming at them. "Hi."

"Did you really meet Ivy Baxter in Hawaii?" asks one of the girls. She has hair as pink as bubblegum.

I have to pinch myself occasionally, wondering if everything in Hawaii really did happen the way the newspapers say it did. In a funny way, I remember more about the million newspaper articles after the event than I do about the actual meeting-a-megastar bit. Although I'll never forget how I was stuck under the bed when one of the world's best-known, bestselling musical artists came into my apartment to talk to me. "Awks" doesn't really cover it.

I get a flash memory of Ivy's bright green eyes sparkling, sharing a joke as we danced around that hotel terrace for our Hawaiian photo shoot. "Being a star is fun, but it's also hard, Storm," she told me. "But just because something is hard doesn't mean you can't manage it. I know *you* can." That's what I call a slightly better memory.

"Of course she met her," says the second girl, whose hair is as green as her friend's is pink. The two of them remind me of the ice-cream combo in Belle's bowl. "She sang on the same stage as Ivy, didn't she? I saw you at Ivy's gig, Storm," she adds, smiling shyly. "I mean, I watched that clip of you on YouTube. You were amazing."

Hearing her say that sends me right back to that incredible Hawaiian stage, opening a gig for a megastar, in the middle of all the dry ice and stage lighting. My jacket is pink and my hair is big and I'm singing ... singing...

"Ow!"

Belle has kicked me under the table. My fans exchange glances. Apparently I've been spacing out. And humming my song. I need to claw this back.

I point at the ceiling of the ice-cream parlour. I hum a few more soaring bars in my best Jennifer Hudson voice. I add a couple of head thrusts for effect.

"Just, you know," I say in the most normal voice I can manage, "practising. Got to practise, right? I'm recording some new songs at the moment. For my album."

I think I've got away with it. The girls relax.

"Um, cool," says Pink Hair. "Can we have a photo?"

"Sick," says Green Hair. "Can you sign my T-shirt?"

"*Practising?*" says Belle when the Ice-Cream Girls have left.

"I panicked, OK?" I take the last scoop of my ice

cream before it melts into total slush. "You shouldn't have kicked me."

"You shouldn't have been staring off and humming like a crazy person," Belle returns.

I groan, laying my head on the table.

"You just lay in a blob of peanut caramel."

Best friends. Who'd have them?

I sit up as Colin Park comes into the parlour. His jacket collar is turned up against the wind and his cheeks are pink. His hair looks like it's been through a tumble dryer, with his overlong fringe blown up and over in a startled-owl kind of way. I feel the peanut-caramel ice cream dribbling attractively down my cheek and wipe it away as quickly as I can.

"How did you know we'd be in here?" Belle says as Colin pulls up a chair next to her.

"It's Friday afternoon, where else would you be?" Colin says cheerfully. "Hey, Storm."

I wipe my face again in case I missed a bit of peanut. "Hey, yourself," I say because I'm a wizard at banter.

Colin Park isn't exactly cute, although he isn't uncute either. He's tall and thin as a twig, and although his trousers are always a bit too short, he somehow gets away with it. I'm still dealing with the fact that he's going out with Belle. It's all a bit weird, having two of my friends date each other.

"Want an ice cream?" Belle asks. "It's on Storm."

"Literally, I see," says Colin, eyeing my face.

The dang peanut is still there.

"So I'm doing some recording next week, Colin," I say when I've wiped my face AGAIN and a chocolate-banana combo has been ordered for Colin and I've photographed it and tweeted it and hashtagged it even though chocolate and banana completely don't go together, in my humble opinion. The parlour owner smiles and gives me a thumbs up from behind the counter. "And I have these new songs that I'm desperate to lay down," I finally continue. "My style has really come on since my experiences in Hawaii – it's much more mature and professional. I wrote three tracks the week I got back. It's unbelievable how fast they came. It was like they couldn't wait to get out."

"Like you in Mr Todber's algebra class," says Belle.

I ignore her. "So I've booked some studio time at Spacebar on Tuesday afternoon and I've got to record as much as I can," I tell Colin. "We only have five hours. It's unbelievably expensive and it's really difficult to book; they don't take just anyone."

I ignore Belle's raised eyebrow. "Hey, do you want to hear the songs? This one's my favourite. *Dance with me,*" I begin, closing my eyes. "*Dance so close and you will see, flowers twining through the beat, dance with me and feel, OH, feel that heat. . .*"

"That'll be you standing too close to the radiators," says Belle.

I open my eyes. I feel extra irritated when I see that Colin is trying not to laugh. "There's no need to take the mick," I say. "You know how important this is for me, Belle."

Belle sighs and gazes down at the pinky-green remains of her ice cream. "Sorry," she says. "It's just... You're a bit full-on with all your stuff at the moment, Storm."

I have literally no idea what Belle is talking about.

"*Stuff?*" I say. "It might be stuff to you, Belle, but it's my *career.*"

"Not yet it isn't," Belle says.

I have a good mind to tell her to buy her own ice cream in future. *No apologies.* I take out my phone to give me time to regroup. There are LOADS of notifications. I soothe my ruffled feathers by scanning through them.

Spacebar Studios @spacebar100
Guess who's paying a visit next wk? #storm
#music #album #watchthisspacebar
@stormhall_official

Jenny Coggan @bubblgum
Just seen @stormhall_official eating ice cream!!!

Mario @mariosmagicsprinkles

Best customer @stormhall_official in today! Try
our new choco-chilli combination! #icecream
#storm

Storm Hall @stormhall_official

👍 to Mario @mariosmagicsprinkles! Done it
again! Might write a song about you one day ☺
#music #storm

Within moments my tweet has seventeen likes.
I feel better.

"When did you change your Twitter handle?"
asks Belle.

"I haven't changed it," I say. "I've just got a new
account for career purposes. @stormhall_14 wasn't
working as I'm fifteen now. Plus I want something
that will work later, when I get famous and there'll be
lots of fakers trying to impersonate me." I playfully
stick my tongue out at Belle. "Look, I have to go.
See you later, loads to do for next week's session. It
has to be perfect, you see. Quick selfie?"

))

Belle and Colin squish up so I can photograph us all in one go.

"Move over a bit so I can get the Mario's Magic Sprinkles logo in the back," I instruct. "And all together . . . strawberry sundae!"

CHAPTER 2

The song isn't coming together as well as I would like. But maybe I'm being too hard on myself. There's only so much that a hairbrush, two shoeboxes and my sister can manage.

"Can't you make the beat more Hawaiian?" I ask Tina in frustration, lowering my hairbrush microphone. "A bit more palm-trees-in-the-wind and breeze-in-the-hair so it goes like this: *Dance with me – ra-ta-ta-ta – dance so close and you will see – ra-ta-taaa...?*"

Thunk-thunk-thunk Tina goes on the long, thin, deepish-sounding knee-boots box. *Dum-dum-dum* on the smaller, higher sandals one. *Dum-da-da-dum.*

"Not like that!" It's so annoying when you can't get across what you want. "You just sound like someone crashing around the footwear in Sports Direct."

"Oh cheers," Tina says, looking put out.

I start scrolling through my phone looking for a beats app I can adapt. "Forget it," I say, waving irritably at her. "I'll do it some other way."

Tina gets up and salutes. "Yes, ma'am, Miss Megastar, ma'am," she says. "Idiot," she adds as she leaves my room.

I can feel the beat so clearly in my head, all sultry and warm and pulsing. I hope Spacebar Studios have drums we can use for the beat. I mean, my life savings are going into the deposit for the studio hire, so they better! I look up their website again and am relieved to see that they do indeed have drum kits and guitars available for recording use.

"Mum!" I yell, hurrying down the stairs. "Dad!"

"What?" says Dad, appearing from the kitchen.

"Who's playing drums for my recording session at the studio on Tuesday?"

"His name's Rory McKee," says Dad.

"Is he well-known?" I ask. "Is he in a band? Have I heard of his band?"

"He was in a band once," says Dad. "My band, actually. The band I had at university. We were called Caffeine."

I contemplate the enormous cup of coffee in Dad's hand. Figures.

"Your uni band?" I say doubtfully. How old is this Rory guy?

"He's a terrific musician, Storm," Dad says. "He's worked with all the greats."

I brighten. That sounds encouraging. "Who?" I ask. "Nile Rodgers? Marvin Gaye?"

"Kia-Ora," Dad says. "In about 1984. He did Um Bongo too. He seemed to specialize in soft-drink commercials in those days."

I am still sitting at the bottom of the stairs with my head in my hands when Mum comes in.

"Homework done?" she asks when she sees me.

"Mum," I say, not about to get knocked off track for something as unimportant as homework.

"Dad's got some really old guy doing drums for my recording on Tuesday. It's going to be a nightmare. Can't you do something? I need someone young and funky to get the right sound."

"Rory's great," says Mum briskly. "Cheap too. I notice you haven't answered my question about homework."

My mother has *weird* priorities.

"It's kind of done," I say.

Mum raises her eyebrows. "Kind of done," she repeats. "As in not, in fact, done at all?"

I don't get why she's so obsessed with homework. I bet big stars like Jase Mahone and Selena Gomez don't have to sit around at weekends doing algebra or reading comprehensions.

"As in," I say reluctantly, "done *in my mind*. I don't get why I have to write it down. Isn't it enough to know it?"

Jake and Alex zoom past the bottom of the stairs, yelling. Jake is wearing an Iron Man mask and silver trousers. Alex is wearing my old tutu and has a toy car in each hand. It's not clear which game they are playing, but they are playing it loudly.

"Until those standard examiners figure out how to mind-read, you do, unfortunately, have to write things down, Storm," Mum says when my little brothers have disappeared into the living room. She gives me her special Mum look. "I don't want any more letters from your teachers telling me your mind is 'elsewhere'. You are still in full-time education whether you like it or not. You have to figure out a way of balancing your schoolwork and your music. If you don't, it won't be the schoolwork that gets cut."

Great weekend this is turning out to be.

But I give it one more try.

"Mum," I say, "it's really important that we talk about Tuesday's session before I—"

"Do your homework," says Mum, disappearing into the kitchen. "Now."

I trail upstairs. If my drummer is a hundred and four, I wonder glumly if my guitarist is on a Zimmer frame. How am I supposed to concentrate on homework with this looming over my entire future?

My phone beeps.

Shopping trip? I need an emergency outfit!!! B xx

Interesting.

What kind of emergency? I type.

A Colin emergency!! He's taking me to the cinema l8r!! Bxx

Lucky Belle, I think. No one's taken me to the cinema in AGES. Or, more accurately, EVER, unless you count my parents.

Babes, cinemas are dark. Sure you need a new outfit?

Her answer comes back at once.

We're meeting beforehand so I need to look good!!! I know where 2 go, it closes at 4, can you meet me asap?

"Your homework still needs to be done!" Mum shouts as I run out of the door twenty minutes later.

"I'll finish it tomorrow!" I shout back. It's hard shutting the front door with crossed fingers, but I manage it somehow.

Belle is waiting for me when I get off the bus.

"That's quite an outfit, Storm," she says.

I look down at my silver jumpsuit, my cinched-in waist, my red quilted bomber jacket and my boots. I matched my lipstick specially to my jacket. "Going shopping for clothes is a serious business," I inform her. "Have you noticed that you get better service if the shop assistants can see that you've taken extra trouble with your appearance?"

"I guess," says Belle.

I look her over. "You look good too," I say. "Maybe

a bit understated though. But don't worry. I've done the overstating for you."

I pull down my sunnies and check my reflection in the bus station window. Not bad, if I say so myself. I got three photos on the bus on the way in.

"Right," says Belle, after explaining where she wanted to go. "If we take the shortcut round behind John Lewis, we can cut across George Square—"

"It'll be quicker if we head down Buchanan Street," I interrupt, "and take a left a bit further down."

The little man is green. I adjust my glasses and walk over the road towards the shopping centre cut-through.

"Wait, Storm," says Belle, coming after me, "Buchanan Street is going to be busy and I really want to—"

"Are you Storm Hall?"

Twenty seconds into the mall and someone's recognized me. That's good going.

"Yes," I say, smiling happily. "Hi. I'm out shopping

with my friend today. Hey, Belle, come over here and get a photo!"

Belle joins me. We smile together and pull faces for the girls' phones.

"It would be great if you could tweet that and copy me in, OK?" I say to the snapper. "Thanks. Ooh, Belle, check out that window!"

"Storm, I really want to go to that shop I told you about," Belle says as I nip across the crowded mall to gaze at an awesome studded jacket in the window of a mall boutique.

"Babes, we totally will. Now that jacket would look *amazeballs* on you. Let's try it on."

By the time we've both tried the jacket on, a little crowd of people have gathered by the shop doorway, peering in. A few people take pictures.

"I wish they'd go away," says Belle as we hang the jacket back up.

"You get used to it," I tell her. I smile and wave and there's a little flurry of flashes. "Now, that shop you wanted to visit. Let's go!"

It's easier said than done, to be honest. There are

a lot more people now, all wanting to take pictures. Maybe the silver jumpsuit was a bit full-on for a Saturday afternoon in Glasgow.

"We're never going to get there," Belle frets as we finally emerge into the daylight on the other side of the mall.

"We will," I say confidently. "What's the dress like?"

"It's red, and kind of short," Belle begins.

"Oh my gosh, it's Storm Hall! It is you, isn't it?"

"Sorry," I say to Belle, pulling a face as three more girls snap pictures. "Kind of goes with the territory. Yes, hi everyone, just out shopping with my bezzie, that's her over there!"

A few people swing round to stare at Belle before swinging back to me.

"Is it true you're going to record with Ivy?" someone asks.

"Excuse me," says Belle in a loud voice. "We're shopping here. Can you go and bother someone else?"

"You didn't have to be rude to them," I protest as

Belle hustles me on down Buchanan Street. "These people are the ones who'll buy my records."

"And I'm the one who needs to buy that dress! Did you come this way on purpose?"

I smooth down my bomber jacket and wave at a couple of guys who nearly walk into a lamp post. "Of course not," I say. "It's just normally quicker going this way. Oh, hi! Yes, of course you can have a picture! Tweet me, OK?"

Belle stands to one side as I let a few more people take some pics. "If the shop closes before we get there, Storm, I'm going to be SO mad at you," she says.

"It won't be closed," I say confidently.

It's closed.

Belle folds her arms and taps her foot on the pavement as I peer hopefully into the dark interior of the shop. I rub my ear. Oops. Where did all that time go?

"OK, so it's closed," I admit. "My bad." I eye the dress in the window. "But you know what? I have a much better dress you can wear back at home. Do you want to come back to mine?"

"Right now?" Belle says flatly. "No."

"Go on," I plead. "I really am sorry about the shop. I got some incredible clothes last week, you'll love them."

Remember perk number two I told you about? Free stuff? It goes way past ice cream. I get jackets, jeans, shoes, hats, bags. All I have to do to keep them is tweet about them.

Belle weakens. "Good stuff?" she says.

"Completely the best. I mean, seriously designer," I say. "There's this incredible little gold dress that would be totally killer on you. Come back to mine and I'll style you."

"Fine," says Belle reluctantly. "I guess Mum'll be glad I haven't spent anything."

"Exactly," I say, feeling relieved that she's forgiven me. "We'll just take the bus back to mine and— Oh, hi! Yes, it's me, yes! Of course you can have a picture! Only don't take too long, OK? I have to get my mate back home to get ready for the date of her life!"

"You're a nightmare, Storm," Belle mutters as I pull her up the road and back towards the bus station.

"I know," I say, giggling. "But you still love me, right?"

CHAPTER 3

"So let me get this straight," I say, lolling on my bed as Belle parades around my room wearing the gold dress. "Colin kissed you, or you kissed him?"

Belle smooths the dress dreamily. It looks sensational on her, just the way I knew it would. "It was a bit of both," she says. She turns and looks over her shoulder at the back view. "After the National Choir Finals, we had a bit of a party and we kind of danced. . ."

I raise my eyebrows. "Either you danced or you didn't, babes."

"I danced and Colin shuffled," Belle says, giggling. "He's the weirdest dancer, but in a very cute way. Do you have any shoes to go with this?"

I rummage in my cupboard for the right pair of shoes. While I'm looking, I imagine Colin Park dancing. Waving his arms around like seaweed, maybe doing the knee-swapping thing they do in the Charleston. Weird, yup. Cute?

"And so one minute we were dancing and the next minute we were kissing." Belle grins, selecting a pair of strappy black sandals from the pile I've heaped on the bed. "And I can confirm that he's better at kissing than dancing."

"You and Colin, *snogging*," I say when we have finished snorting. "I still can't get my head round it."

Belle stops throwing shapes at the mirror and looks at me. "You're OK with it though, right?" she says.

"Of course I'm OK," I say, feeling startled. "Why wouldn't I be OK?"

Belle lifts a shoulder. "I guess a few of us always thought maybe you fancied him a bit?"

I sit bolt upright. "I could *never* fancy Colin! Never in a million years!"

Belle looks a bit offended. "Are you saying he's ugly?"

"Of course not! It's just . . . me and Colin . . . I couldn't imagine. . . He's not really my. . . I'm not really his—" I stop and breathe and rewind. "What do you mean 'a few of us' thought I fancied Colin?" I say, extra appalled. "Who's 'a few of us'?"

"Just me and Jade and Bonnie and Sanjit and Daniel," says Belle.

Just? JUST? Nonononono. EVERYONE thought I fancied Colin? How much worse can this get?

"Oh," Belle adds, "and Colin too."

I can feel myself turning green.

Colin Park thought – maybe still thinks – I fancy him.

"It was the cat emoji, wasn't it?" I say when I can breathe again. "That stupid cat emoji I sent him from Hawaii. I knew that would come back and bite me. I only sent one, and for no reason, OK? And it's totally not the same as sending a message that says 'I fancy you, Colin'!"

Belle is studying herself in the mirror from all sides. "If you say so. Storm, this really is an incredible dress, and the shoes are perfect. Are you sure I can borrow them?"

I wave my arm at the clothes bursting out of my wardrobe and clear my throat, which feels like it has a whole pond of frogs in it. "What are best friends for?" I say. "Of course you can. So, what time are you meeting him?" HIM. COLIN PARK. WHO THINKS I ONCE FANCIED HIM.

Belle checks her watch. She squeals.

"In about fifteen minutes," she says in horror. "How did it get so late? When's the next bus into town?"

"In fifteen minutes," Tina says, passing my bedroom door. She's glammed up to the – not even the nines, actually, the tens or maybe the elevens. "I'm heading that way myself."

"Dad'll give you a lift," I say, springing into action, bagging up Belle's clothes, which are scattered around my bedroom floor.

Tina looks relieved. "Great. These shoes are

already killing me and I've only made it halfway down the landing."

"I'm not talking to you," I tell my sister as I hustle Belle down the stairs, slinging her bag round her shoulders as we go. "Come on, Belle, you can't be late for Colin after all this. Dad? DAD! Can you give Belle a lift into town? It would totally save her life!"

Dad gives Belle *and* Tina a lift in the end. ("But only because I'm almost out of coffee pods for the machine and the only place that stocks the decent ones is in town. This isn't going to be a regular thing, OK?") It's a relief when the car lights pull away. I need some time alone, to think about how completely unaffected I am by the news that practically my entire school year think I fancy Belle's boyfriend.

Sunday morning. I sit up, peel away the cucumber slices that I put there on Saturday night (they are dry and crusty but amazingly they stayed on all night), stretch out for my phone and snap a cheeky little "Morning, world!" for Instagram. It's terrible so I get out of bed, have a shower, wash my hair, condition my hair, extra condition my hair, exfoliate everything, moisturize everything, put on some make-up, put on my PJs again and get back into bed. Click! Better. I add the right filters and upload.

Playing dress-up with Belle last night has put me in a dress-up mood today. I fling open my wardrobe with enthusiasm. Half of it jumps out and hits me in the face.

"You wanna play mean?" I challenge the jumble on the floor. "I can style myself with my eyes closed and you know it."

I do a mic drop for another snap, then literally jump into the pile of yumminess. Tees, skirts, jeans, playsuits, jackets, belts. I roll around for a bit taking pictures. It's fun, until it all turns to static and I end up with a load of tees stuck to my head. I dust myself off and stand up reluctantly.

Ivy's pink jacket smiles at me from deep in the hanging part of my wardrobe. *Storm, you have to do whatever it takes*, she had said. I take it from its hanger. Too much for a Sunday? *Be the star you want to be, no matter what anyone else says.*

I check my social media feeds. Fifty-seven likes on my "Morning, world!" already and it's only just gone nine thirty! Fifty-seven likes officially makes this a pink-jacket day.

Jake and Alex both choke on their cereal when I make my entrance.

"No pictures, please," I say, striking a pose in the kitchen doorway.

"Fine by me," Tina says.

Alex is wearing my old tutu again, and his bicycle helmet. His toy cars are, as usual, parked by his glass of milk. "I'm the Tinkerbell Stig," he says, looking at me with interest. "What are you?"

I flick my sunnies down from the top of my head so they land just right on the end of my nose. "A rock star, Al," I inform my littlest brother in my best drawl.

"Coco Pops or muesli?" says Dad.

"Avocado on toast, please," I say, sitting down beside Tina.

Dad looks mystified. "You want an avocado for breakfast?"

"Dad," I say, "avocado is packed with twenty different vitamins and minerals and it's super good for your skin. Miranda Kerr swears by it."

"But last time we had avocado you said it tasted of mushy frogs," says Dad.

Jake makes a ribbity noise. Alex laughs. I wave my hand. It jingles, thanks to all the rings I'm wearing.

"That was then," I say with dignity. "This is now."

Dad finds an avocado right at the back of the crisping drawer in the fridge. We only have Homepride white toast, which I don't think too many celebrities eat, but it will have to do. I smear the avocado – well, kind of slice it, really, because it's as hard as a stone – and try to squash it on to the toast. The toast disintegrates. I fold it up as un-crumbily as I can and tuck it into my mouth and chew. It had better be as good for your skin as all the celebrities say.

"Cup of tea?" Dad offers. "You know, to take the taste away?"

"I'd rather have coconut water," I croak. "Rihanna drinks it every day."

"Of course," says Dad. "I'll just go and pick a coconut from our coconut tree."

"Storm, stop being a plonker and have a normal breakfast and a cup of tea," says Tina.

"Thank you, Tina, I couldn't have put it better myself," says Mum. "There's still a bit of Nan's marmalade left in the bottom of that jar, but you'd better be quick or I'm going to have it."

I fiddle with the mesh crop top I've got on under the pink jacket. It's a little colder in the kitchen than I was expecting.

"I bet Ivy drinks coconut water," I say. "Did you know that a glass of coconut water has more potassium than four bananas?"

Mum pushes the fruit bowl towards me. There are five bananas in it.

"Oh," Dad adds, splashing my tea with extra milk. "As the last one down for breakfast, Storm, you're on dishwasher duty."

"I can't load the dishwasher in these," I protest,

lifting my jingling fingers. "Anyway, washing up stuff makes your hands wrinkly and rock stars never have wrinkly hands."

"Dear Lord, what have we created?" Mum mutters at her paper. "I hate to ask this question, Storm, as I think I know the answer, but have you done your homework yet?"

I am suddenly, furiously fed up. *No one takes me seriously in this house*, I think. *No one understands me AT ALL.*

"No, I haven't done my stupid homework," I complain. "Because, as I think I've told you before, it's boring and I still have to practise for the recording session on Tuesday, or have you forgotten about that? Who *cares* about school?"

Mum lowers her newspaper.

There is a dreadful silence.

Dad busies himself with the cafetière. Jake makes a face. Alex puts his hands over his ears. Mum only ever puts the paper down on a Sunday morning if someone's in a LOT of trouble.

Oops.

"I think I'll go somewhere else," says Tina, standing up.

"Storm Hall," Mum begins in her darkest, deadliest voice as Tina leaves the kitchen at speed. "You will not speak to me in that manner in my house."

I attempt to say something, but Mum's faster.

"You WILL eat your breakfast, which your father and I have worked hard to provide, and you WILL remove all of that make-up and that outfit, which are both completely unnecessary on a Sunday morning, and you WILL do your homework in the kind of clothes that don't restrict the flow of blood to your brain."

"Mum, I—"

Mum hasn't finished.

"You will do all of these things by lunchtime today or I will cancel your recording session at Spacebar Studios."

I gape at her. She can't be serious. This is my FUTURE we're talking about. We booked that studio weeks ago. It's practically impossible to book it any less than six weeks in advance. If Mum cancels, I won't be able to record anything for another SIX WHOLE WEEKS. Six weeks before I can begin my search for a record deal. Six weeks. . .

"You wouldn't," I say.

Mum narrows her eyes.

"Try me," she says.

CHAPTER 4

"So I did my homework by eleven thirty," I tell Belle in a low voice. It's Monday and we're at the back of our chemistry class, making quite a good job of hiding behind the Bunsen burners as Dr Macallister prowls around looking for kids to put in detention. "Because there is no way on this EARTH that I'm not going to record my songs tomorrow night. Can you believe she threatened that?"

"Your mum can be really scary," Belle says.

"She's completely terrifying," I agree. "And you know the worst thing? She doesn't seem to GET it. Which is crazy, seeing how she's my manager. Whoever heard of a manager not wanting their client to succeed in the music industry? It's hard enough out there without your manager being out to get you too."

"I'm sure your mum isn't out to get you, Storm."

"Yeah, well, that's what it feels like," I grumble.

"So..." says Belle, lifting her eyebrows at me.

I pull my thoughts from brooding revenge and try to work out why she's looking at me so expectantly. Do I have toothpaste on my cheek? Hollywood dermatologists have started advising their clients to use toothpaste on blemishes because apparently it works just as well as expensive creams. I gave it a go last night. Have I forgotten to wash it off?

"Aren't you going to ask me, then?" Belle says.

"Ask you what?"

"About my date? With Colin? The gold dress?"

"OH my gosh!" I gasp. "How was it? What was the film? How was the dress?"

"You'd forgotten about it, hadn't you?"

"No! It had just ... got pushed behind a couple of other things, that's all." A couple of things like my annoying mother and three pages of algebraic equations and the lilting rhythm of "Dance with Me", which I still don't totally have down.

Belle sighs. "The dress *was* a bit over the top for the Renfrew Street Cineworld, but I loved wearing it. Colin said it was like sitting next to a well-wrapped toffee."

"That's a compliment, right?" I check.

"If it's not too much trouble to have your attention, Storm and Belle?" hisses Dr Macallister.

Belle and I sit forward and fix our eyes on the whiteboard. I last about five minutes before I'm checking my phone for social media updates. I mean, it's important to stay on top of these things. *Do whatever it takes.* I hum a snatch of "Dance with Me". I think I've figured out the rhythm problem. It all needs to go slower.

Storm Hall @stormhall_official
Can't wait to record my new tracks
@spacebar100!! You're going to love them!
#music #bigtime #love

I scroll idly through the rest of my feed, liking a few things as I go. I pause on mega-hottie rock phenom Jase Mahone's latest post, which features an eye-catching ad for his upcoming tour.

Jase Mahone @jasem4real
Extra d8 y'all! Now gigging GLASGOW this w/e!!!!! Hurry and get those tickets #reddeviltour
♺ 42k ★ 78k

I feel my heart rate speed up. Jase is bringing his tour to Glasgow? This weekend? Belle and I *have* to go! Will there be tickets? There *have* to be tickets. I lose myself in a yummy fantasy about getting tickets to Jase to celebrate my massive record deal—

"I'll have that if you don't mind, Storm."

Dr Macallister has materialized at my side. He is glaring.

This is not good.

"Sorry, sir," I say hurriedly. "I was just updating something."

Dr Macallister's grey, hairy eyebrows scuttle up his forehead.

"It would appear," he says, removing the phone from my fingers, "that I need to update YOU, Storm, on the school policy of using phones during lesson time."

"But, sir—"

"No buts, Storm. You are not a goat."

My phone disappears inside Dr Macallister's large lab-coat pocket.

"The problem, sir," I say, doing my best to stay calm, "is that I get hundreds of notifications every single day. If I don't stay on top of them, my phone will literally explode. It's been proved, sir." Has it been proved? I wonder in distraction. Chemistry isn't one of my strong points. I just HAVE to get my phone back.

Dr Macallister turns his head to the watching class.

"Hands up those of you who believe that social likes can cause a chemical reaction of the magnitude required to blow up a phone."

Jade Miller puts her hand up. She puts her hand down again when she realizes she's the only one.

"I'm not alone, then, in doubting your 'proven fact'," Dr Macallister says, turning back to me. "You can collect the phone at the end of the day, Storm."

"Please, sir," I try again, pulling my most innocent expression. "You don't understand—"

Dr Macallister's eyebrows go even higher than normal. "No, Storm, it is you who doesn't understand. School policy. No exceptions. And I don't want to hear another word, or you'll get detention."

"But, sir, I *really* need my phone," I insist.

Dr Macallister huffs in exasperation. "OK, then, detention tomorrow afternoon," he replies.

The urgency about my phone now pales into total insignificance. Tomorrow? I can't have a detention tomorrow. Tomorrow is the day of the recording!

"Sir—" I gasp. I'm close to tears now.

"Good Lord, Miss Hall, are you angling for more trouble?" Dr Macallister snaps. "Detention tomorrow. Here. With me. And, in case it's not entirely clear, do NOT use your phone in my class ever again."

Belle watches me with worried eyes as I pace up and down the corridor with her phone pressed hard to my ear at break. Mum can fix this, right? Mum fixes everything.

"Poor little Storm Hall," smirks Emily Douglas, hockey queen of Endrick School, shoulder barging me as she passes down the corridor. "Looks like you'll have to do your little recording into your phone instead of at Spacebar Studios. I hear there's an app that can make a donkey sound like it's singing. It'll be perfect for you."

"Hur hur," says Emily's twin sister, Gwen, running her hockey stick along the lockers right beside my head. CLANGCLANGCLANG.

I flush and glare. I don't want to say anything in case Mum picks up the phone when I'm swearing at the Hockey Horrors. She doesn't take kindly to that kind of thing, and I need her in a good mood for what I've got to tell her.

Emily and Gwen walk on down the corridor, laughing. Belle pulls a sympathetic face at me just as—

"Meggie Hall speaking."

"Mum," I say, "I really need your help. Dr Macallister gave me a detention tomorrow afternoon, and it was totally unfair. I can't miss the recording. Please can you talk to him? Please?"

"Oh, Storm," says Mum. I cringe at the disappointment in her voice. "What did you do?"

"I was using my phone in his lesson, but it was just for a second, I swear. Could you just explain the situation to him? He wouldn't even listen when I tried to tell him about the studio."

"No."

I clutch the phone a bit tighter. "Please, you have to!"

"I don't have to do anything, Storm," says Mum, quite gently by her standards. "You are the one who has to abide by the rules. You're already turning into a diva, and we haven't even got you a record deal yet. It worries me."

"I'm not a diva! I'm a singer, and I'm doing whatever it takes to make it. I'm under a lot of pressure, and no one is giving me a break. I'm asking for your help!" Tears are going to come, I know it. I can feel them itching at the back of my eyes. My lovely recording. My beautiful songs, my life, my entire WORLD . . . it's all going up in smoke.

"If a detention is what it takes for you to control your behaviour, then a detention is what you'll have to have. I'll call the studio, see if we can reschedule the recording," says Mum, sealing my fate. "Try and learn something from this, will you, love? I'll see you later."

I make one last effort to change her mind.

"But rescheduling will take WEEKS! I could do the detention on Wednesday instead. If you call Dr Macallister and explain, I'm sure he'll—"

But. . .

Click.

Mum has gone.

CHAPTER 5

I stare miserably at my beans on toast. It might as well be bird droppings on a roof tile.

"Eat up," says Dad. "They'll go cold."

I fix my family with dark and savage eyes. "I'm *grieving*."

"It's only a recording session," says my sister.

"Only?" I demand in fury. "That was my life right there, Tina. And now it's been ripped away from me thanks to a science teacher with badgers for eyebrows."

"I *think* you'll find it was because of your behaviour, Storm," says Mum.

I fold my arms and stare bitterly at the table,

brooding on the disaster of my life. Detention today was like water torture. Drip, drip, drip. Staring at the clock and imagining all the songs I should have been laying down. All the riffs, all the perfect improv moments, all the magic. Dr Macallister didn't even notice the laser look of death I trained on him for the entire hour. What a waste.

"I'm going to my room," I say, standing up dramatically.

"If you're hungry later, you'll have to make do with an apple," says Dad as I stalk out of the kitchen.

I stop, seize the apple, glare at the room and continue on towards my bedroom. Nobody understands what it's like to want something the way I want this. Or maybe they do, and they're just jealous that I'm actually trying to do something about it.

My music is good, really good, and a lot of people would get a lot of happiness out of it. I just need to get it out there. But it's like the world is conspiring against me.

Storm Hall @stormhall_official
Bad day. Really bad. The worst. I hate my life.

My finger hovers over the button. Should I send this? I don't want to worry my fans, even though it would be kind of nice to know that SOMEONE out there is feeling my pain. It's more than anyone's doing round here.

I delete and rewrite.

Storm Hall @stormhall_official
I could really use some #mariosmagicsprinkles right now! #badday

I check out the rest of my feed for a bit. No more updates on Jase Mahone's Glasgow gig, but plenty of retweets I notice. Tickets are going to be tough to get. Tough, but maybe not impossible. I let the Jase poster on the back of my door (complete with lipstick kisses) soothe me for a bit, then I text Belle.

Jase's gig on Sat. As dedicated MaHunnies, we should totally go?

Tickets are sold out, I already tried L Bxx

I'll tweet that I want some tx, you never know!!!!

Dream on, rock star!! Bxx

I tweet a jokey request anyway. Then I scan through a bit of fashiony stuff. A few pictures pop up of me and Belle from Buchanan Street at the weekend. We look pretty good, and I cheer up a bit more as I read the comments.

Jasmina Ahmed @jasminaaaah
So cool meeting @stormhall_official at the weekend!!!! Wanna hear a new song NOWWW!!! #music #storm

Billy Green @ladzagogo
.@stormhall_official in town looking AWESOME.

The lamp post didn't hurt that much #idiot
#staring

Resting my phone on my chest, I lie down on the bed and eat my apple morosely and stare at the ceiling, listening to the *ping ping ping* of my notifications button.

There's a knock on the door.

"Can I come in?" says Mum. Coming in.

"Doesn't look like I can stop you, does it?" I mutter.

Mum sits on the end of my bed. "I've rebooked the session," she says.

"For about five years in the future, right?" I ask, bracing myself. Everyone knows Spacebar Studios is impossible to book at short notice.

Mum smiles. "Happily for all concerned, they had a cancellation for a week on Friday."

I sit up so fast that my phone slithers off my tummy and on to the floor. The notifications are muffled by the carpet and now sound more like *bungbungbung*.

"Really?" I say through my apple. My heart has turned from a gloomy stone into a soaring butterfly in one go. "A week on Friday? Can the drummer guy do it? Can the guitarist?"

"Yes, they're all free," says Mum.

I fling my arms round her. "Thank you, Mum! You're the BEST!"

"You're rubbing your wet and sticky apple core against my neck."

I deal with the apple and fling my arms round her again.

"Please tell me you've learned your lesson," Mum says, stroking my back.

"Completely," I fervently tell her shoulder. "I will give Belle the *strictest* instructions about warning me the next time Dr Macallister is on the prowl. He's never going to get me again."

"Not quite the lesson I was hoping for," Mum sighs.

"I mean," I adjust, giving my fantastic, wonderful mother my most winning smile, "of COURSE it won't happen again. I will give Dr Macallister – in fact, I will give ALL my teachers – my full and undivided attention for ever."

Mum doesn't look as if she believes me. "If it happens again, Storm," she says, "I won't rebook, do you understand? You almost lost your deposit today, and your dad and I aren't going to pay for it if you cancel again."

I feel a little *glump* of guilt. "It's all my pocket money for the last two months."

"Right. Pocket money you're not going to get now for the next two months," Mum says.

I'm so happy about Spacebar Studios – a week on Friday is only is only ten days away – that even the thought of being cashless for eight weeks can't bring me down. Anyway, what's eight weeks' pocket money when I have a whole LIFETIME of megastar megabucks waiting for me? I'll pay Mum and Dad back a thousand times over when I hit the big time. I want them to know how grateful I am for everything that they've ever done for me. Woo-hoo! The career plan is back on track! Take that, Dr Macallister!

Downstairs, the doorbell rings.

"Who on earth can that be?" says Mum, detaching herself from my octopus arms. "It's a little late for a postal delivery."

We both look over the banisters and down into the hall, where Dad is talking to a guy in a blue cap on the doorstep. Tina, Jake and Alex are all peering curiously round the living-room door.

"Storm!" Dad calls. "Delivery for you!"

I've received freebies a few times via delivery guys since my Ivy gig, but they don't normally turn up at seven o'clock in the evening.

"It's probably avocados," says Tina from the living-room door. "They're calling to you, Storm, listen. 'Tweet about us, Storm Hall! Tweet "hashtag avocados are great"!'"

"Ha ha," I sigh, taking the envelope from Dad's hands. It doesn't look like it contains avocados at least.

The envelope is thick and pure white, with my name written in big, curly, green letters on the front. Turning it over curiously, I slide my finger under the flap. A pair of tickets, complete with holograms and the Red Devil logo, slide out, together with vouchers for a personal shopping experience at Topshop and a makeover at the Taylor Ferguson salon. But it's the handwritten note that catches my eye.

Dear Storm. You wanted tx? You got them!
Jase xx

CHAPTER 6

"I was only *joking* when I tweeted about wanting some," I say feebly as we all stare at the tickets in my hand. "I never thought I'd actually *get* them."

Tina carefully takes the tickets and vouchers from my hand. We all follow her into the living room, where she props everything up on the mantelpiece for all of us to see. We gaze at them for a bit. Even Jake and Alex are totally quiet, and it takes a lot to shut them up.

"Jase Mahone has touched those tickets," Tina says in a hushed whisper.

"It was probably his PR team," says Mum.

I'm having an out-of-body experience right now.

Has Twitter suddenly developed magic powers? Not only do I appear to have two tickets to the hottest show in town, I also have a handwritten note from Jase Mahone. STORM, he's written. And two kisses. JASE xx.

"Let me see that envelope," says Mum.

I hand over the envelope. I can't take my eyes off the tickets. VIP, they say. That means backstage.

"There's an address on the back," Mum says. "Echo Music."

And backstage means. . .

"That's Jase's record label," I say, swallowing.

Backstage means I might meet Jase himself.

I have to tell Belle.

Belle the most incredible thing everevereverever has just happened CALL ME!!!!

My phone rings practically before I've sent the text.

"I got tickets," I blabber at Belle before she's even asked me what's going on. "I've got VIP tickets and shopping vouchers and a pamper treatment at Taylor Ferguson and—"

"Slow down, Storm. What's going on?"

Jase's face swims into my line of vision. Bleached, tousled hair. Blue eyes. That cute overbite, that broken nose, that cheeky love-heart tattoo he has just below his right ear. "I've got tickets for the Jase gig," I burble. "From ACTUAL JASE MAHONE."

Belle's shriek makes me pull my phone from my ear.

"OMG, Storm, are you SERIOUS? JASE sent them? He knows who you are! OMG, he actually KNOWS WHO YOU ARE?"

My total teen crush knows who I am. How weird is that?

"You are going to take me, right?" Belle begs down the phone.

"Babes, of *course*! Who else would I take?"

Tina, listening-but-pretending-not-to-listen, looks crushed. My first thought is: she shouldn't have teased me about the avocados. My second: ever since we first screamed at a Jase video, and drew love-heart tattoos on each other's necks, and did our best-ever dance routine to his classic track "Knock Me Down", it was only *ever* going to be Belle who came with me to a Jase Mahone gig. I pull a sympathetic face at Tina.

"How does he know where you live?" asks Dad as I interrupt Belle's screaming with a hasty "talk to you later" and hang up.

"Dad," I say, "he's Jase Mahone. Multimillion-dollar megastar. He can find out *anything*." I can't believe I'm having to explain Jase to my dad. Where's he BEEN for the last three years? "And the gig's this Saturday. So I can go, right?" I pause, and rephrase. "I mean, please may I go?"

"I'm not sure you should be going anywhere after your behaviour this week, Storm," says Mum.

I swallow back a snappy "Are you serious? This is JASE we're talking about!" retort. After the day I've had, no way I'm risking this amazing opportunity with a cheeky attitude.

"I know I've been a nightmare this week," I say humbly. "I completely deserved today's detention and I'm so sorry that I almost wasted the deposit money at the studio today. I really truly have learned my lesson. And I'll even do my homework on Friday evening to prove it, right after school."

Dad nearly chokes on his coffee. "Friday?" he repeats, looking at Mum. "Not Sunday night? Not first thing on Monday morning?"

I shake my head, clasp my hands together. "Friday right after school," I repeat firmly, pushing all thoughts of Mario's Magic Sprinkles out of my head. "I'll come straight home and I'll do *everything*. Just – please, *please* can I go to the gig?"

"There's some washing up left over from dinner," hints Dad.

"I'm on it," I say at once.

"And your room hasn't been tidied for about three months," Mum adds.

"I'll tidy it! I'll even vacuum!"

"Well. . ." Mum's thawing. I can tell.

"Everything will be done," I say. I put my hand solemnly on my heart. "I swear it by my ENTIRE trainer collection." (That's about as serious as it gets.)

"Fine," says Mum at last. "But if you put a foot wrong this week. . ."

"I won't!" I jump in. "I promise! Thank you, thank you, you're the best parents EVER!"

I'm already redialling Belle to discuss outfits as I head for the washing-up with a song on my lips and little tweety birds of happiness whizzing around in my stomach. Even icky saucepans hold no fear for me tonight.

I'm going to see Jase. IN FOUR DAYS' TIME!

CHAPTER 7

"The red or the blue?" Belle asks.

"The red is brilliant with your hair," I say.

"So I should go with the red?"

I take a snap of my ice-cold sparkling water with its slice of lime. It looks super-Arctic against the white-and-Plexiglas table. "Definitely," I say as I upload the pic. Which hashtags should I go for? #topshop #sparkles #jase should do it.

Belle twirls on the spot, holding the jacket – a sensational military-style one with brass buttons and a cute nipped-in waist – close. "I love it," she says happily. "What about you?"

"I'm going to try on the blue one again," I say.

I clamber out of the squashy white sofa – harder than it looks – and reach for the jacket Belle just put back on the long steel rail. It's the same style as Belle's, but in an amazing bluebell shade.

"You told me you liked the red so you could have the blue," accuses Belle, laughing.

I grin as I slip the jacket on. She's kind of right. "Red did look better on you," I say. "Honestly! Selfie?"

We preen and pose in our jackets – one red, one blue, identical in every other respect. I match the jacket with a pair of shoes so high they practically send me into orbit. Snap, snap, snap. Belle takes some pics too.

"I can see those before you upload, right?" I say.

"If you want," she says, handing me her phone.

I flip through the pics. "Not that one," I say. "My chin looks awful. What filter are you using? Nope, that one's awful too."

"It's a good one of me," Belle protests.

"But it's totally AWFUL of me," I repeat patiently. "Use this filter, it's great with my skin tone."

I press a button and upload the pic.

"But—" says Belle.

"Sorry, too late," I say cheerfully. "You could take some of you with your filter but I'll stay out of it." I wave at the assistant. "Could I please have some more water? With a bit more ice this time? Thank you!" I turn to Belle. "You know, that jacket really does look incredible with your white dress. Jase is going to love it."

Belle looks dreamy. "I can't believe we're going to actually see Jase up close," she says. "It's like one of those dreams I had when I was twelve."

"I KNOW," I say, and we squeal like rocket balloons for a bit.

Right now, life is pretty awesome.

It's a short taxi ride to Taylor Ferguson for hair and make-up. *Three hours to go*, I think as we settle down in the salon's big comfy seats. Three hours till we're standing backstage with Jase Mahone himself. The selfie opportunities are going to be MEGA.

Nails: long and red, of course, with Jase's Red

Devil symbol painted on each one. Hair: I go for long and sleek. By the time the stylist has finished with me, I feel like a glossy racehorse. Belle goes for a side bun, which looks adorable. Mum sits with a magazine while Belle and I settle down with the MAC make-up consultant.

"Big night, then?" asks the girl looking after me. Her name badge reads "Gwenie".

"The biggest; we're going to the Jase Mahone concert," I say. Gwenie is looking at me like she's trying to work out whether she knows me, so I decide to give her a hint about who I am. "Well," I add, "maybe it's not quite as big as the time I met Ivy Baxter. . ."

"I knew I recognized you!" Gwenie says, her face brightening. "Steel, right?"

Belle laughs beside me. I feel a bit annoyed. Cheeky mare!

As Gwenie and Belle's girl – Ella May – finish our make-up, Belle reaches over and squeezes my hand.

"You know," she says unexpectedly, "I'm so proud of you."

I beam at her. "You've never said that before."

"Well, I may not say it again. Your head is way too big as it is."

I'm still feeling quite bruised about the Steel thing, so I pull my hand away, my irritation rising.

"Excuse me?" I say.

"Well, everyone is too nice to you."

That doesn't even make SENSE.

"How can anyone be TOO nice?" I demand. "Isn't it *nice* to be nice?"

"Not *all* the time," Belle says cryptically.

I feel a flash of anger. I'm giving Belle an amazing evening. Doesn't she realize?

"Maybe I should have brought Tina tonight," I snap.

Belle's eyes widen. "What?"

I pull out my phone and play with my feeds for a bit to calm myself down.

Storm Hall @stormhall_official
Incredible VIP time @Topshop and
@HairGlasgow tonight ready for @jasem4real
go #reddeviltour!!

I pause as I read that. He can't mean me, can he? He *might* mean me. I look over at Belle to ask her what she thinks. Her head is bent over her phone and her fingers are whizzing.

"Who are you texting?" I ask, forgetting that we just argued.

"What do you care?"

O . . . K. She's still mad at me. I feel a flash of anger again, deep in my belly. This is an experience of a lifetime. Shouldn't Belle be acting a bit more grateful?

"Belle, I'm talking to you," I say, grabbing her phone.

"Doesn't mean I have to listen," Belle returns, grabbing her phone back. "Where do you get off talking to me like that?"

"You started it!" I protest. "You said I had a big head!"

"You do!"

"I do NOT! Who are you texting?"

"Colin, if you must know."

I might have guessed. It's always Colin with Belle these days.

"Nice to know your boyfriend is more important than spending time with me," I snipe.

"Nice to know you're online when you should be talking to ME!" Belle whips right back.

"I have to do updates, it's part of my career!"

Mum looks up from her magazine. "Is everything OK?"

Belle and I breathe heavily at each other.

"We're fine," I say after a moment, even though we're not fine at all.

Mum closes her magazine. "Good," she says. "Just time for a quick photo and then you should be off. The driver won't wait."

My anger drops away like a stone off a cliff.

"Driver?" I repeat, glancing at Belle. She looks as astonished as I feel.

Mum smiles. "Didn't you read the small print

on those tickets? A chauffeured car is part of the package tonight. Your youngest brother is very jealous, needless to say."

Proper rock-star treatment! I feel excited all over again as we are positioned for our makeover photos. Gwenie applies powder to my cheeks, and Belle poses beside me, smiling and turning for the photographer. I hope this means we're back to normal.

CHAPTER 8

The ride is over too quickly. I stretch and sigh as the driver glides our Maserati up past the glowing blue walls of the Hydro Arena towards the VIP entrance. We drive through a throng of Jase fans, all wearing Red Devil T-shirts, and I catch a glimpse of their faces as we purr through.

"They're wondering if we're Jase," I say, peering out through the smoked windows.

"I could get used to this," says Belle.

"Stick with me, baby," I say in my best New York accent, and Belle laughs.

"Miss Hall?" A guy in a tight-fitting black T-shirt

opens the door of the car. "Welcome to the Hydro. May I see your tickets?"

I feel a bit awed as we climb out of the Maserati. There's a red carpet and everything. Cameras flash. Belle sticks close to me. I can tell she feels weird as well.

"Storm! Over here!"

I'd forgotten how high these Topshop heels are. I teeter a bit before I can get my balance, but once I'm there, I'm posing, holding my jacket lapels, twisting my hips the way Ivy showed me in Hawaii ("It always makes you look slimmer, darling"), making pouty faces as the cameras flash away.

"Who's your friend?" someone yells.

I realize I've forgotten Belle in the thrill of my red-carpet moment. I turn to look for her, and see that she's got herself wedged between two burly security guys. I beckon her and, after a moment, she comes out with a shy smile.

"This is Belle," I announce. "My best friend in the world."

"Love the jackets!" someone else shouts, and we

both laugh and put our arms round each other – and suddenly it's like all our fantasies, practised for hours on our bedroom carpets, turning and posing and pirouetting for the cameras as the photographers go crazy.

"That was SO fun," Belle says as the security guys move in smoothly to usher us through the VIP entrance as another fancy car swings into view. "Oh, Storm, let's not fight any more, I hate it."

For some reason I want to cry. But I don't because that would smudge Gwenie's gorgeous MAC make-up. I hug Belle tightly instead.

"We won't," I say. "I promise. Come on, Jase is waiting."

Yup. There go those rocket balloons again.

The atmosphere is already incredible. We are shown to the reception area of the VIP lounge, where a girl wearing heels even higher than mine smiles with perfect red lips and offers to show us to our seats. We're right on the edge of the action, perched above the crowds as they filter into the mosh pit at the foot of the stage, with plush seats and a table set with soft drinks, sparkling water, crisps and a cute bowl of Starbursts. Red lights strafe the stadium from end to end; roadies rush around the stage like ants in headphones.

"Oh man," says Belle, sinking into her chair and grabbing a handful of crisps. "What a view."

"Remember the last time we were here?" I say.

"To see Ivy!" says Belle, and we share a smile. "We were at the side of the stage, weren't we? And we thought *that* was good. This is something else."

I've already taken out my phone and am snapping our seats, our goodies, our view. I snap Belle and even remember to add the filter she likes before I upload it with a hundred excitable hashtags like #besties and #swag and #style and #jase and #magic. I gaze longingly at the stage, at where the dry ice is already starting to swirl around the set. Not much longer, I tell myself. When I've recorded my tracks at Spacebar and got my record deal, I'll be up there too. Singing for the world once again.

"What are you thinking about, Storm?" Belle asks softly.

"My future," I say. "I know I'm only at the very beginning of my career, but I just know I'm going places. I can almost touch it."

Belle offers me the sweets bowl. "You can touch a Starburst for now."

I stick out my tongue and pick out a pink one. And then. . .

The lights go down. We swing round to the stage, transfixed, as something rises from the centre of it. It's a huge trident lit in red neon, and someone is holding on to one of the great black prongs in a red jacket with a bare chest and a set of horns on his head. It's. . .

"JASE!" we scream.

"JASE!" scream forty thousand other fans.

"*Knock me down*," Jase Mahone sings as that familiar bass line kicks in.

"*Send me low*," we sing back. "*Kick around until you know, don't let it go-go-go, don't let it back, don't let it crack, knock me . . . knock me down.*"

I'm doing the moves. Belle's doing them too. Grapevine left and grapevine right, pump the fists and grind the hips. . . We're twelve again and we're laughing like we haven't laughed in AGES.

"*Knock me, knock me,*" Jase sings, sticking out his chest and holding his fists in the air. How he's still on that trident, I do not know.

"*Dow-wow-wown, dow-wow-wown,*" cry the fans. "*Knock me, knock me down!*"

We dance until we can hardly stand as track after classic track blasts through our brains. At some point I kick off my shoes. This is wild. This is amazing. This is. . .

Over.

The lights flash on the last encore, and it's clear after a full ten minutes of screaming that Jase isn't returning to the stage.

"Water," Belle groans.

I'm so sweaty I can hardly pass her bottle without it slipping through my fingers. Gwenie promised that my MAC mascara was super waterproof, but after the beating I've just given it, who knows?

"I look like a panda, right?" I gasp as I sweep my sweat-soaked hair out of my eyes.

"How 'bout a selfie now?" Belle grins. Her hair has come out of her neat little side bun and is spilling all over her shoulders.

"NO selfies," I agree, giggling. "Not before a repair job."

A girl appears behind our seats, making us jump. It's the girl from the reception desk, the one with the mega heels. Her lipstick is still perfect.

"Miss Hall?" she says. "Jase would like to meet you. If you'll follow me, I'll take you backstage."

Belle and I exchanged an appalled look. Meet Jase looking like we just went through a sweaty, crisp-stained carwash?

"Um," I say in panic. "Can we just, er, freshen up?"

I've never been so relieved in my life as when the girl smiles and shows us to the bathroom. A vision of hell greets me in the mirror. I've lost a button on my top, and my hair – well. Let's say "glossy racehorse" doesn't really come to mind. More "dog that's just been through a very large puddle". The mascara is about the only thing that's held up. Belle and I get the most awful giggles as we try to tidy ourselves. We're about to meet Jase and we resemble two crazy-haired lunatics.

"How do I look?" I hiccup after five minutes' frantic brushing and powdering. I'm breathless with laughter and nerves.

"A cross between wild and cool. Me?"

"Glowing," I say. "But incredibly. Not in a sweaty way." I swallow and lick my lips. "Ready?"

Belle takes a deep breath. "As ready as I'll ever be," she says.

We follow Red Lips down a carpeted corridor that's way too quiet by comparison to the crazy show we just watched. My heart is hammering loudly in my chest and I keep thinking I'm going to wake up as we reach a door with the words JASE MAHONE stencilled in gold. Belle is shivering with excitement beside me. This is a dream, right? I'm not actually going to meet—

"Hi, Storm. I'm Jase. I can't tell you how glad I am that you came tonight."

I stare into Jase Mahone's blue eyes as his familiar growly American voice washes over me. Gawp at his broken nose. Blink at his love-heart tat. And fall off my heels and have to grab him by the shoulders to keep myself upright.

"Wimble," I squeak into his startled face.

I JUST FELL INTO JASE MAHONE AND SAID WIMBLE.

He laughs and sets me back on my feet. "Great shoes," he says.

I JUST FREAKING FELL INTO JASE.

"Yes," I say, trying frantically to recover. He probably gets this kind of thing from fans all the time. Maybe they even get as far as a face plant on his dressing-room floor. "I fall off them all the time. I'm a health and safety nightmare."

Jase grins. "Who's your friend?"

"Belle. As in ding dong?"

What am I saying? I don't even know what I'm saying. Belle blinks a bit at her introduction but manages to stay upright, at least, as she shakes Jase's hand.

"Hi." She sounds so much cooler than me. "Really great to meet you."

Sweeping his blond hair out of his eyes, Jase nods at Red Lips, who produces a bottle of sparkling water from somewhere. Cold drinks are pressed into our hands. I want to roll mine against my forehead to cool myself down but I resist.

"Did you enjoy the show?" Jase asks, offering me and Belle a seat on the squashy red sofa set against the wall of his dressing room.

"We LOVED it," Belle and I say in chorus.

"We're dedicated MaHunnies," I add adoringly. I really hope I can get out of this sofa elegantly when it's time to leave. "We've been following you for years. I can't believe you sent us those tickets. It was so kind of you."

"It's a great show," he says, sitting down beside me. "My technicians are superstars, and I have some terrific people behind me. Echo Music really are the best in the business. Listen, Storm, I meant it when I said how great it is that you came to my show. I love your music."

Belle and I exchange a shocked glance.

"You've heard my music?" I say.

"Of course," he says, like it's the most natural thing in the world that Jase Mahone with his twenty million Instagram followers should know about my music. "You have an incredible voice."

"Thanks," I say ecstatically. "So do you."

He looks at me appreciatively. "I love the look," he says. "Want to take a photo?"

I glance at Belle, who just stares wordlessly back. Jase appears to be flirting. With ME.

We snap a shot, Jase's bangled arm extended right out in front of us with his other arm looped around my shoulder. He puts the phone down and fixes his gaze on mine. It's as if Red Lips and Belle aren't even in the room.

"You're pretty cool, Storm Hall," he says.

"I don't feel very cool right now," I say, staring at him.

"The coolest people never do." He gently tweaks a bit of my hair. "We should get together. Do you want to swap numbers?"

CHAPTER 9

"Be careful, Storm."

I add some fresh MAC mascara. You can never have enough of the stuff, in my opinion. Gazing back at me from the mirror in Jase's private bathroom, my eyes are as sparkly as two glitter balls. Jase Mahone is flirting with me and I'm flirting back. Talk about starting at the top. I've picked a guy the whole world has a crush on and I'm going with it and it seems to be working out pretttttty well.

"Careful of what?"

"I don't trust him."

I put the mascara away and look incredulously

at her. "This is *Jase* we're talking about. Jase who a million girls completely ADORE, us included. What do you mean, you don't trust him?"

Belle frowns. "Call it a feeling."

"Don't spoil this," I say. "Jase is into me. I can't believe I'm saying it, but it's true. I can *feel* it. Right here." I pat the place where my heart feels as full as a can of fizzed-up soda.

"Is that where you keep your vast experience of boys?" Belle asks.

I don't like the tone of her voice. It's sharp and spiky and it reminds me of when we argued at Taylor Ferguson's. Was that only a few hours ago? It feels like a LIFETIME. I will always think of my life in terms of before and after now, I think dreamily. Before I met Jase, and after.

"I may not have been out with many guys," I say, "but—"

"You haven't been out with ANY guys!"

This is a small and unnecessary detail.

"Well," I say defensively, "I'm starting with the best, then, aren't I? Belle, I may be fifteen, but he's into me. You heard the things he was saying, about my look and my great smile and everything, right? Didn't Colin say stuff like that to you?"

"Colin told me my teeth made him think of a giraffe," says Belle. "He loves giraffes."

I wish I hadn't asked now.

"And that is better than being told I'm cool by the coolest megastar in the world?"

"I'm not saying it's not great that he's saying all these things," says Belle. "I'm just saying, don't believe everything he's saying. If you know what I'm saying."

I don't.

"We have to get out there again or he'll think we've fallen down the toilet," I say.

Jase is on the phone when we step back into the dressing room.

"Talk later," he says into the receiver, then hangs up. "Storm, you look more gorgeous than you did when you went in there. How is that even possible?"

Belle snorts. I decide to kill her later.

"Thanks," I say with my best and most sultry smile as I settle back into the sofa.

"I've had a huge crush on you for months," my teen heartthrob now tells me. I'm glad I've already sat down. "Ever since I heard you at Ivy's gig. I was there, you know."

He was?

"You were?"

"Incognito, of course." Jase looks deep into my freshly mascaraed eyes. I try not to blink. It's like looking into the sun. "Your voice, it's just so . . . *mature.*"

"I was only fourteen," I say, and then wish I hadn't because I don't want to give Jase the impression that I am in any way too young to be girlfriend material for a seventeen-year-old guy.

"Unbelievable," says Jase, shaking his head. "I've listened to your songs, like, a hundred times."

"The ones I sang for Ivy?" I ask eagerly. "Which was your favourite? Was it 'California'? Or—"

Jase takes my hand. I stop speaking mid-sentence because I literally have zero words.

"I loved them all," he says. And he kisses my hand.

I am never EVER washing my fingers again.

"We'd better go, Storm," says Belle.

Jase is twisting his fingers through mine like long brown worms. No, wait, that sounds gross. They're more like ... Jase Mahone's fingers. Yes. Jase Mahone's fingers and my fingers. Together.

So.

Cool.

"Your mum said the driver would be here at half past ten," Belle says loudly. "Jase, it was a great gig and it's been an incredible experience meeting you. Thank you so much. Storm? Let's go."

She has physically pulled me off the sofa and out of Jase's grasp. I feel like a fish that's just been plonked on a dry and arid shore. He looks a bit shocked.

"It's not that late, Belle," I try, but Belle is now talking to Red Lips, who is opening the door. Jase is saying something but I don't catch it because the door shuts behind us.

"Phew," says Belle, leading me down the corridor. "I thought I was never going to get you out alive."

I yank my arm away from her. "What do you think you're doing?" I hiss in fury. "It was going really well in there!"

Belle grunts. "A bit *too* well. It makes me wonder what the guy is after."

Ah. AH! The penny – finally – drops. How could I have been so slow?

"You're jealous!" I say. "Jealous that Jase Mahone fancies me!"

Belle rolls her eyes. "I'm not, believe me. We're tired and it's been an amazing night, but enough's enough. It's like, two boxes of chocolates: fine. Three: not so fine. If you know what I'm saying."

I hate it when Belle gets cryptic. I cling to the one thing I'm completely certain of.

"You're jealous because you've only got Colin and I've got Jase," I spit.

Belle whitens. "You talk rubbish sometimes, Storm," she says.

I put my arms round myself. Even with my fab Topshop jacket on, I'm suddenly feeling cold. "Talk about dog in the manger!" This is one of Dad's favourite expressions and one I never thought I'd find myself using. "You've already got a boyfriend, but now you want mine as well."

"Jase Mahone is not your boyfriend, Storm," says Belle.

"Not yet, maybe, but he could be one day! He took my *number*."

"The car's here," is all she says back.

I can't enjoy the ride home, this time in a Mercedes-Benz. Belle's spoiled everything. Jase might even have kissed me if she hadn't stuck her busybody nose in. I feel faint at the thought of kissing Jase Mahone. It would have felt like kissing a unicorn.

OK, that didn't come out right: I don't actually want to kiss a unicorn.

My phone beeps.

So great to meet you, Storm. I'll call you. Jase xx

He's attached the photo we took together on the sofa. I sink into the wonderfulness of seeing his handsome, famous face snuggled up so close to mine. We're both grinning like anything. Two kisses on his text too. No cat emojis for this guy. He's a *grown-up*. I want to show it to Belle so we can scream about it together, but I'm not going to give her the satisfaction. I can't believe she isn't letting me enjoy this. Why can't it be real? Love happens all the time, everywhere you look. Why can't it happen for me and Jase? Why does he have to be "after" *anything*? Apart from me, that is.

The Mercedes pulls up at Belle's house.

"Thanks for nothing," I snarl. "And don't think for a minute that—"

Belle gets out and shuts the door before I get the chance to finish my sentence, so she'll never know what for a minute I didn't want her to think.

I plonk myself back furiously on the plushy seat. How can I feel like crying after one of the best nights of my life? I can hardly see the screen on my phone as I send a message back to Jase.

Jase, I had the best night ever.

I'll never forget it in a million years.

Storm xx

Shame you had to leave!

I had plans. . . J xx

What plans??

You'll never know now!

I'll call. I promise.

J xx

CHAPTER 10

"Are you coming or what?"

I'm definitely not imagining it. Belle is still annoyed with me about Saturday. It's unbelievable. I gave her the best tickets to the best show in town and introduced her to one of the most famous, gorgeous rock stars in the entire world and she's treating me like a piece of boring gum stuck to the bottom of her shoe.

Two can play at that game.

"I have. To get. My phone," I say, in an extremely slow voice.

She knows this, for goodness' sake. She was even with me when I handed my phone in to reception this morning to make sure I wasn't tempted to check my messages – oh boy, would I have been tempted – and got myself another detention and the cancellation of Spacebar Studios on Friday.

She gets this sour look on her face like she's bitten into a lemon and checks her watch. Colin lurks by the doors, clearly keen to stay out of the tempest brewing between me and my so-called bestie.

"The bus leaves in fifteen minutes," is all she says.

"I KNOW." Extra exaggerated. "I've only been catching it for . . . ooh . . . my entire LIFE. Didn't you hear me? I need. To get. MY PHONE."

"If you hadn't been dawdling down the corridor letting the entire school snap photos of you, you'd have it already."

I bite the inside of my cheeks. The photo session had been fun.

"I expect your 'boyfriend' has missed you," Belle adds snarkily.

"I can totally hear the quote marks on that," I say. "Don't think that I can't."

"We'll leave without you if you're not coming in five minutes, Storm."

I practically snatch my phone from the receptionist's outstretched hand. What if Jase has been texting me all day and I haven't replied and he thinks I'm not interested and he gets with Willow Smith who I know is totally into him or what if Saturday and all those texts on Sunday were a dream and—

STOP, I order myself as my phone slooooowly turns itself on. *You are getting carried away.*

Jade Miller bounces up to me. She's a bit like a King Charles spaniel, all big brown eyes and happy face. "STORM!" she squeals. Squealing is Jade's default setting. "I can't BELIEVE what happened to you at the weekend!"

I adjust my face so that it broadcasts the right level of pleasure. Happy but not screaming about it. That's how a real rock star would do it.

"It was pretty cool," I say modestly.

"COOL?" Jade squeals. "Are you SERIOUS? You and JASE!"

A couple of other girls stop by the reception desk on hearing Jase's name.

"Laura told Daniel who told Sanjit who told my sister's best friend who told my sister you actually met Jase Mahone." Bonnie Lawrence's eyes are narrowed like she can't quite believe it. "Everyone's saying that it's true."

"Maybe you should check out my Instagram account," I say with a coy smile.

"I ALREADY DID!" Jade squeals. "THERE'S A PICTURE OF YOU AND JASE!"

More people have joined us. We're a bit of a squeeze in reception now. I'm enjoying myself enormously. *This is more like it*, I think. I glance at Belle. She and Colin are deep in conversation and don't even look round. Typical.

"Did you get his number?" demands Bonnie.

I waggle my phone and smirk.

"Did you kiss him?"

"He kissed my hand," I tell them. "No biggie."

Everyone gasps and stares at my fingers like they're made of gold. Bonnie's eyes narrow a bit more.

"Oh, and he texted me loads over the weekend," I add airily. "I haven't checked today because I've only just got my phone but there are probably a few messages waiting for me."

Jade's face is a picture of awe. "Check now!" she says. "I want to see what he's written."

I look at my screen. Mentally punch the air about a hundred times. Hold the phone up for my audience.

Missed you today!
J xx

Can't wait to see you again!
J xx

"J could be anyone," says Bonnie as everyone screams on cue.

"It's got his PICTURE on it, Bonnie!" Jade is almost dead with excitement. "On the message. Storm, another message is coming in! Is it from Jase?"

U got style Storm Hall!

Jase xx

"OMG," Jade moans. "Jase Mahone FANCIES you."

I give in to an overwhelming desire to show off. (Well, wouldn't you?) "What can I say? It was like electricity when we met. He looked into my eyes and – bang."

"What, he shot you?"

Bonnie's almost as bad as Belle.

"It was love," I inform Bonnie a little stiffly.

"I can't take any more!" Jade screams. "I literally can't stand it!"

This has been fun, but Jade's starting to give me a headache.

"Gotta catch my driver," I say as Jade grabs me round the waist and snaps a picture of us together. "Kidding! I mean, my bus. See you in the morning, superstars! Love you!"

Belle and Colin aren't by the double doors any more. I check my watch. The bus goes in four minutes. It dawns on me that Belle's done exactly what she said she would. She's left without me.

I break into a run, charging down the steps outside school, clutching my phone with my Jase messages on it like it's a lifebelt. *Superstars shouldn't have to run for buses*, I think as I swerve past staff members pulling out of the car park, tragic music blaring from their open windows. It goes against all the laws of nature.

"Belle!" I'm pounding along the pavement now; my bag is bouncing uncomfortably on my back. "I said I was coming! Why didn't you wait?"

Today of all days, the bus is flipping early! What are the chances? Is the entire world ganging up on me? I avoid a kid in a pushchair by half a millimetre and practically hurdle over a litter bin.

"WAIT!"

I catch the bus just as the doors hiss shut, and I have to wrestle for a moment to get my whole body inside. My eyes are stinging with sweat. I can feel a blister swelling inside my shoe. Everyone on the bus is staring at me, and for all the wrong reasons.

Belle and Colin are sitting in their usual place.

"Why didn't you wait?" I demand. Except it comes out as, "Why (gasp) didn't (heave) you (pant) wait?"

"We waited as long as we could," says Belle.

"You *didn't*—"

I stop because my phone is ringing. Fixing Belle with my 'This isn't over" glare, I hold it to my ear.

"WHAT?" I snap.

"It's good to hear your voice too, Storm Hall," says Jase. "I think."

I sit down suddenly. So suddenly that I land in Belle's lap.

"Storm," Belle protests. "You're squashing—"

"*Jase!*" I squeak, waving at Belle to be quiet. "It's you! You're calling me!"

"Yes, it is, and I am," Jase confirms. "Why haven't you returned my texts?"

My heart is no longer a heart. It is an elephant

rampaging around a very small room, i.e., my ribcage, trying to get out.

"I only just got them, honest! I had to give my phone in at school and I just picked them up!"

I hope Belle can stand me sitting on her lap for a bit longer because I don't think my legs are going to work. I also wish I hadn't mentioned school. It makes me sound way younger than I really am. (In my soul, I mean.) Jase Mahone is calling me ON THE BUS.

"You've had me on edge all day!" To my horror, Jase sounds a bit annoyed.

"I really am sorry!" I'M ON THE PHONE TO JASE MAHONE I want to tell the bus, the street, the whole entire world. "I'll send you a message now if you like!"

He laughs, which is a relief. "I'd rather talk to you. So when are we going to hang out?"

I don't know how many more capital letters my brain can take. JASE MAHONE WANTS TO HANG OUT WITH ME.

"Depends where you are," I say, catching my

breath and doing my very best to be cool. People are staring at me and whispering. One or two have their phones out. It's great but not so great too. I need to concentrate on my conversation with a megastar.

"Dead leg, Storm," says Belle loudly.

"Who's dead?" asks Jase.

"Belle," I say. "I mean," I amend, struggling, "she's not really dead, that would be weird because that would mean I was talking to a corpse." *Nice recovery*, I think. *NOT*. "Her leg," I say, "is dead. Because I'm sitting on it."

"You're full of surprises, Storm Hall."

"I guess I am," I say. "OW!"

"The dead leg just injured you?"

"In a manner of speaking," I say, scrambling out of the footwell where Belle has dumped me. "Listen, it's so great talking to you, but could we talk later?"

"I'm in LA right now," he says, like he's just round the corner.

"That's good, right?" I check. "Your time zone is behind us so I can call later?"

"*Exactamente*, baby."

Belle acts like she's not listening, but she rolls her eyes at this. *Exactamente*, I think, is *exactamente* what I'm going to say from now on every single time Belle annoys me.

CHAPTER 11

Jase Mahone @jasem4real

Hangin' online with my new super talented BF
@stormhall_official @EchoMusicLtd #music

Storm Hall @stormhall_official

Getting down with Jase! If only IRL!
@jasem4real ☺ #music #alwaysthemusic

Luisa Lopez @MaHunny1

Te quiero pase lo que pase 😭😭😭
@jasem4real #jase

I have kept my promise not to look at my phone during school hours all week. Now it's Thursday, there's one day to go until our recording session at Spacebar Studios, and I'm FaceTiming Jase Mahone.

Yes. You read that right.

I never get tired of watching him push his famous blond hair out of his eyes. He's squinting a bit because it's summer in LA (it's never anything else) and he looks extra cute. With FaceTime, it's like watching my favourite gif on a loop.

"... so of course, my feng shui element being water, I'm like, don't give me dry ice, man! That's so contrary! But my stage manager, he's like, we cannot stage a waterfall on the Red Devil tour, Jase, you'll drown the fans."

Last night Mum made me hang up after an hour and fifty-three minutes. This is the trouble with handing in your phone from nine till three every day. We always have SO much to catch up on.

"And you know the green hat I wore during 'Fight Free' at the Glasgow gig? That sequence when I fought off those neon ninja guys?"

"That was unbelievable," I say enthusiastically. "It was totally my favourite—"

"I wasn't allowed to wear that hat when we toured China. A green hat means I'm cheating on my girlfriend. The Chinese fans would NOT like that, I can tell you."

Am I his girlfriend now? I wonder. I feel like his girlfriend, even though he's in LA and I'm in Glasgow. We talk and text ALL the time. I think of him ALL the time. (Except when I'm eating cookies and then I think about the cookies.) If that's not love, what is?

Jase is still talking.

". . . and as for the trident, you know the colour red is, like, hugely significant in China? It originates with fire. But you know what you get when you mix fire and water?"

I think about my science lessons. "Steam?" I venture doubtfully.

"Extinguishment."

Is that even a word? I wonder.

"I had a lot of therapy to get past this fear that if I set foot on that trident I would go out like a candle," he continues.

This sounds a bit weird, but Jase looks so serious about it that I don't crack an inappropriate joke.

"Couldn't you have made it blue?" I suggest instead.

"I wish! Only the tour was called Red Devil, so. . ."

I feel a bit stupid. Jase sees me looking crestfallen.

"Don't worry about it," he says kindly. "You just have stuff to learn about this business; it doesn't happen overnight."

He brushes his hair out of his eyes and squints some more in the bright LA sunshine. I glance out of the window at the Glasgow night. It's not really the same.

"I wish you lived over here," I say. "Then at least we'd be in the same country."

Jase grins his extra-twinkly grin. "How much do you want that?"

"More than *anything*. It would be so great to actually see you." *And touch you,* I think, feeling a bit giddy at the thought of holding Jase's hand.

He winks at me down the webcam. "I might just be able to grant that request, Storm Hall," he says. "I'm thinking of moving to London."

My mouth falls open. Remembering that I'm on FaceTime and Jase can see my every move (no nose-picking permitted) I start speaking at once so it doesn't look as if I'm just gawping like an idiot.

"Uuuhh, that would be incredible, really?" I stutter. "You'd do that?"

He kisses the tip of his finger and presses it to the

webcam. For about half a second, all I can see is his fuzzy pink fingerprint.

"Anything for you, Storm," he says when he has removed his monster finger from my vision. "My people will be in touch with your people real soon. Now I have lunch with Bee and Jay and I'm already almost a half hour late."

I picture two letters of the alphabet eating whatever letters of the alphabet eat in LA.

"Bee and...?" I say, trying not to sound too curious.

"Beyoncé and Jay-Z. Really great people, you should meet them sometime. *Ciao ciao*, baby, be good."

He winks out and I'm left blinking at the screen. There are spots of LA light dancing around in front of my eyes, or maybe that's just stardust. Bee and Jay. Bee and—

"TIIIIIIIINA!" I screech. "GET IN HERE NOW!"

"Going out," says my sister, trudging past my door.

"But Jase is having lunch with—"

She's already gone. I snatch up my phone and hit Belle's number. She can't stay cross with me when I've got news of such epic proportions as this.

"Belle!" I say when she answers. "Guess who Jase is having lunch with?"

"Nice of you to call," Belle replies. "Where have you been all week?"

"Busy," I say, determined to keep going with this conversation no matter how hard Belle tries to derail me. "Guess properly!"

"Sheesh, Storm, how do I know? I haven't spoken to you in days."

I start humming "Crazy in Love".

"I ... give up, what is that?"

I'm starting to get annoyed now. "It's 'Crazy in Love', you idiot."

"You're not the only one who gets crazy in love, Storm," says Belle. "Although you are perhaps more crazy than most. Is this important?"

"Of course it's important! I—"

"Only I still have to finish my biology diagram and I'm trying to work out where to put the spleen."

"Jase is having lunch with BEYONCÉ AND JAY-Z!"

It's a shame just to blurt it out, but I can't think of any other way to get it across if Belle isn't going to play Guess Who.

"And you called just to tell me this?" says Belle. "Not to ask me how I'm doing or anything like that?"

I don't get it. How can she not be impressed? I *know* – I am kind of *dating* a megastar who goes round to the house of two more megastars for lunch! I wonder briefly what they're eating. Probably not tuna jacket potatoes, which the Hall household ate two hours ago.

"Are you just pretending not to be interested to annoy me?" I ask.

Belle makes an explosive noise on the other end of the phone. "Storm, you can't just call me after five days of silence and dump famous information at me and expect me to be happy about it. Friendship works two ways!"

"I know that!" I say, nettled.

"Well, it seems like you've forgotten because this has turned into a one-way street," says Belle.

"We've both been busy, you're just reading too much into it!" I have a mental image of me and Belle on a narrow street with motorcycles parked beside a titchy pavement. Maybe with posters along the walls of me and Jase, singing in a swirl of dry ice or maybe under a waterfall. Yes, a waterfall would be good. I . . .

I look at the phone in my hand. Belle has rung off.

CHAPTER 12

"Shall we go for another take? Bernie reckons the reverb on that was kind of muddy."

I tip the headphones off my head and push my hands through my damp hair. No one ever told me that being in a recording studio for hours makes you sweat like a racehorse after the Grand National. Replacing the headphones, I lean wearily into the mic.

"Do you want the whole track again, Gary? Or just the chorus?"

"Better do another full take, Storm, just to be on the safe side," Dad says. "But give us a minute, OK? We're having a few technical hitches."

I glance through the glass window of the recording booth at my parents. Mum is deep in conversation with Gary, the sound engineer. Dad is sliding switches around with one hand and drinking coffee with the other. Tina is hanging around looking bored, although I know she's storing up loads of facts about this place for her mates ("Guess who recorded there? Paolo Nutini! I swear, there's a signed photo on the board and everything!"). The boys are with my grandparents. I miss them, although having them here would be like letting a pair of monkeys loose in a spaceship. The mixing desk is massive and very spaceship-ish, actually. There are so many buttons and dials that it's easy to imagine one of them sending us to the moon.

As Gary and Mum talk about sound quality, I pull out my phone. Still no call from Belle since she hung up on me last night. I can't believe she did that. I'd never do that to her, not in a million years.

I cheer myself up by scrolling through some of Jase's texts from earlier.

))))

LA sucks without you!

J xx

I wish I had a teleporter to bring you over!

J xx

Check out my latest video! http://bit.ly/2ngAPØz

J xx

In the new video, Jase jumps and whirls and does this quick-change thing with his feet. He looks a bit like his trousers are on fire. I feel guilty for thinking that because I should be admiring his technique – which is totally cool, of course – but now I've got the trousers-on-fire thing in my head it's hard not to think of it.

"Ready when you are, Storm," says Gary into my ear.

"Ow!" yells Jase on my phone.

I try to compose myself for the track as I shut down the video and turn off my phone, but I've got the giggles.

"*Dance with me*, ha ha, hooo," I begin.

Mum frowns and Gary looks startled. Rory stops his intro rhythm sequence and Desmond looks up from his guitar. There is an awkward silence. OK, it's not silence exactly, because there's me hooting away like a crazy owl.

"Keep it together, Storm," says Dad mildly, his fingers on the mixing desk.

"Sorry!" I flap my hands and try to get myself under control. Belle would be laughing herself sick round about now and making me worse. I force myself to think of boring stuff like bricks and geography homework. "OK," I say, snorting and wiping my eyes. "I'm with you; can we take it again?"

It happens twice more (EMBARRASSING) before I settle in properly and lose myself in the song. I know I'm home as I swoop through the lyrics. I'm a bird and this is my sky. I belong here. I can't live on the ground. I have to do this *right*. Then Jase will love me even more.

"That sounded great," says Gary when I finish. "In the end."

"We just need to loop it in a couple of places," says Dad, and he starts talking at a hundred miles an hour about ratios of sound and feedback and all the other stuff he's so good at.

My cheeks flush. Proper rock stars probably never get the giggles in recording sessions. I prop myself up against the wall of the booth and close my eyes for a bit as everyone gathers round Dad at the mixing desk. Then I'm summoned to listen to the results for myself. They're amazing. I can't believe it's me.

"Everyone happy?" says Dad.

I nod wordlessly. *I'm so lucky to be here*, I think. I love my life. I've got my family and I've got Jase. The only thing that's missing is Belle. I wish she were here.

Belle is standing outside the studio as we leave. I stop and stare at her. Am I hallucinating?

"I was thinking of you," I say stupidly.

Belle gives half a shrug. "I was thinking of you too," she says.

I am about to go in for a hug when I stop myself. There are things we need to sort out first.

"You hung up on me," I accuse her.

"You were being annoying."

I bristle. "Well, if you're going to be like that—"

Belle holds up her hand. "Sorry," she says. "Storm, can we start again? I've been really worried about you."

I thaw a bit. Like when a snowman gets the first taste of sunshine.

"You don't have to worry about me," I say stiffly. "I'm fine."

Belle sighs. "You want to sing. I get that, really I do. But up till this point, you haven't BEEN singing. You've been on the phone to Jase and taking pictures of yourself and, frankly, poncing around, and it's like the music hasn't mattered at all."

Hasn't *mattered*? What's she talking about?

"I've been RECORDING today!" I say. "Of course the music matters!"

"If it matters, why haven't you been writing more songs?"

"I wrote three!" I say indignantly.

"You wrote those ages ago. All you've been doing

lately is taking pictures of yourself and spending hours with Jase Mahone online. If you're not careful your future isn't going to work out the way you want it to, Storm, because you're focusing on the wrong things."

I throw my hands in the air. "What do you want from me?"

"I want you to be happy," Belle says steadily. "And I want you to be grounded and I still want you to be my best friend. And I'm sorry I upset you yesterday. I miss you, Storm."

My eyes tear up. "I've missed you too," I say, because I have, even though she's the most annoying person in the world sometimes.

"I wish Jase wasn't distracting you so much," Belle says.

I wipe my face because it's wet. "It's not Jase that's distracting me. It's you. I've really missed you, you twerp."

Belle smiles. We hug. We hug a bit tighter. We hug so tightly that we almost fall off the pavement.

"Better?" asks Belle, releasing me.

I sniff and nod. "Better."

"And we won't talk about Jase more than three times a day?"

"I just have to show you his new video," I say, pulling out my phone.

"Oh no—"

"Seriously," I say, grinning, "you have to see this. It's the funniest thing EVER and it completely slayed me in the studio. It was really embarrassing."

I show Belle Jase's fiery dancing. She gets it right away.

"Ow," sings Jase, and she bursts out laughing just like I knew she would, and everything – everything is great and fine and we're hugging all over again and I'm truly, properly happy.

"Storm!" Mum shouts.

She appears to be doing some kind of war dance beside the car.

"Storm! Sound Pacific want to see you!" Mum shouts.

"Sound Pacific?" I repeat. "As in 'we've recorded

every single person you've ever heard of' Sound Pacific?"

"Yes!"

Sound Pacific Records recorded ALL the greats. We're not talking about Um Bongo here. We're talking about Ella Fitzgerald, Lena Horne, Billie Holliday, Dinah Washington. They launched Marvin Gaye. They worked with the Beatles, the Faces, the Clash. Their back catalogue is unrivalled. My entire music collection is ninety per cent Sound Pacific. And they want to meet ME?

"Jase won't believe it," I say faintly. I detach myself from Belle and hold up my phone and snap a picture of myself because I never want to forget how I'm feeling at this moment. I upload it as I walk in a daze towards my family.

Storm Hall @stormhall_official
Watch out @jasem4real @SoundPacific
@thewholeentireworld: A STORM IS COMING
#music

Mum waving her phone around like one of those hi-vis guys on airport runways with their ping-pong bats.

"They're thinking of signing you!" she cries. "They want us in London next week, Storm. Next week!"

"OMIGOSH!" I shout, and I hurl myself at my parents and my sister. "OMIGOSH OMIGOSH OMIGOSH!"

We dance like lunatics around the Spacebar Studios car park. This is it! This is where it all begins! And when we have finished, I look round for Belle, but she's gone.

CHAPTER 13

London! I love it already and we only touched down about half an hour ago. The taxi is purring along and I'm on the back seat playing with my brothers as Mum makes phone call after phone call and Tina turns up her music and peers out of the windows at the London rain (which is of course totally different to Glasgow rain) and Dad tries to engage the cabbie in a conversation about where to find the best coffee in the city.

"Trampoline taxi!" Alex shouts, bouncing his cars off the plush black upholstery.

"Trampoline me!" shouts Jake, undoing his seat belt and getting ready to bounce on the upholstery himself.

"Don't even THINK about it, Jake Hall," says Mum as she dials up another number.

"I'm surprised you're not bouncing on the seat and screaming as well, Storm," Tina says.

"I'm saving my voice," I tell her. "I have to sound my best for Sound Pacific this afternoon."

"I'm looking for that stomach-lining sensation that comes from a proper roast," Dad is telling the cabbie.

"You wanna try my old lady's chicken dinners," says the cabbie.

The rain is thinking about stopping. I can tell. I've built a lifetime of experience out of watching the Scottish weather so that I get my wardrobe right for all occasions. The sky is definitely brightening and I can even see a patch of watery blue hanging around above a gobsmackingly large building with a huge carved stone doorway and ranks of stone animals tucked up against its Hogwarts-esque roofline.

"Natural History Museum," says the cabbie.

Jake stops trying to undo his seat belt. "Is that

the one with dinosaurs? Are we going to see them? I want to see a T. rex."

I check my phone. My last Instagram update has already got over a hundred likes. I lean against the cab window and make a dinosaur face and snap.

Storm Hall @stormhall_official
Watch out, dinosaurs!!! @SoundPacific @jasem4real

"Texting your megastar boyfriend again?" Tina enquires. She teases me ALL the time about Jase.

"You know you're impressed," I tell her.

Tina fakes a yawn.

"Fine," I say. "When I see him, I won't introduce you."

"Don't you DARE," says Tina. She quickly adjusts her face. "I have a responsibility to check out his suitability for my baby sister."

"So it's nothing to do with you wanting a selfie with him, then?"

"Nothing at all. No. Nope. Totally not." Tina

pauses. "Unless he wants one, of course, and then I won't refuse because that would be rude."

Our hotel is down a pretty street of whitewashed townhouses. Quarrel – such as it was – forgotten, Tina and I hold hands tightly as we go into the cool chequered reception, past a huge bunch of flowers that makes Dad sneeze. This place is *awesome*.

Our suite is large and airy with a view of a little garden square. Jake wastes no time in bouncing on the bed with Alex while Tina unpacks her enormous suitcase and me, Mum and Dad make battle plans.

"They're expecting us at two," says Mum, checking her watch. "We have an appointment in the hotel salon at twelve; that should be enough time. We need nails, hair, make-up, the lot."

"They're interested in her voice, Megs, not the way she looks," Dad points out.

"It's all about how you *present* yourself, Bernie." Mum eyes Dad in his dodgy old T-shirt and scrappy jeans. "And anyway, I need a wash and blow-dry myself. So we all have time for a quick lunch and then it's down to business. Clear on the plan, Tina?"

"I take the boys to look at dinosaurs," says Tina with a sigh as Jake and Alex screech and zoom around the suite's shiny parquet floor. "You hang out with music producers. Yeah, Mum, I'm clear."

"I've booked you into the salon as well," Mum coaxes, and Tina cheers up. She secretly likes dinosaurs anyway.

Hi, Jase! We've checked in! Loving the hotel!
Storm xx

Loving your dinosaur face on Instagram.
I'm in London tonight too.
J xx

My fingers go numb. I have to waggle my hand to get them working again.

Which hotel??????

The Billington. Call me later?
J xx

I imagine his blond hair with a shiver of adoration. We're in the same city at last! If Sound Pacific Records like me and sign me, Jase is going to be SO impressed.

We have lunch in the suite and Mum, Tina and I head for the salon, leaving Dad in charge of the boys. I let my thoughts ramble through the flowery fields of fame as they wash and dry my hair. Parties, cool outfits, Jase by my side. London's new power couple. Yes. I like that a LOT.

Mum has lined up a few outfits for me to choose from. Tina eyes the rail.

"Tina can choose first," I suggest.

Tina brightens. "Cheers, Storm. Can I have that grey top?"

"Apart from the grey top," I say. I grin at the look on her face. "Duh, of course you can wear the grey top, Teens. Grey isn't really me!"

We settle on plaid trousers, black heels, a ruffled white blouse and an amazing red jacket. My hair is sleek and my lips match the jacket. I feel a million dollars as we head out of the hotel and climb into the waiting taxi.

It's only as the taxi drives away from the hotel that it sinks in. I'm about to sing for one of the scariest, most influential music producers on the planet. Enrique Diablo doesn't translate as Henry the Devil for nothing. I feel horribly sick.

"You're going to be great," says Mum, patting my hand. "All you have to do is do what you do best. Sing."

I swallow. "Right," I say, nodding. "Sure."

Dad has changed into a suit, which looks kind of weird. "Think of it this way," he says, fiddling with his tie. "What can possibly go wrong?"

My trousers could split, I think in dismay. I could get a frog in my throat. I could sing flat, I could sing sharp, I could sing totally off the beat. I don't want to do this any more. I want to go back to the hotel and crawl under the bed and hide like I do sometimes at home when I'm feeling stressed. I want to go to the Natural History Museum and be the first visitor ever to get eaten by an animatronic dinosaur.

"Hardly helpful, Bernie," Mum says, catching

sight of my face. "Storm, remember this. Enrique Diablo likes what he's heard already. He'll have watched your performance with Ivy; he'll have checked out all your videos and your media feeds. Guys like him always do their research before they get to this stage. All we're doing today is confirming what he already knows. That you would be perfect for Sound Pacific."

I nod, calming down a little. "I could pretend he's Belle," I say.

Dad looks a little surprised. "Do you think that would help?"

"Sure," I say, warming to the idea. "Belle's heard me singing a million times, right? I just have to imagine Enrique Diablo as a fifteen-year-old girl and I'll be totally fine."

"Whatever works for you, love," Mum says. "Ooh, look! We're here."

I concentrate on breathing as we enter the big white cube-like space that is the Sound Pacific reception area. Mum deals with the paperwork, and we get our names clipped on to our jackets. A lady in a black leather skirt escorts us to a swanky white lift, and we cruise soundlessly up to the fifth floor. It's soundless on the outside, anyway. Inside, I'm screaming like a kid on a scary ride at a funfair.

Someone is waiting for us in the fifth-floor lobby, right outside the lift.

"Welcome to London, Mr and Mrs Hall," says Enrique Diablo. He smiles at me. "Welcome to Sound Pacific, Miss Hall."

He is much smaller in real life. I shake his hand and look at his wrinkled, brown face with its expensive set of teeth and do my best to put Belle's face on top of his immaculately suited and booted outfit. This is the guy who signed Amy Winehouse, is all I can think. Who shook hands with Adele at the start of her career, who has more platinum records than any music producer of his generation. Today, I can see the records for myself. They line the walls of his huge office, row upon row of them.

Four people are sitting together by the window, two men and two women. They eye me curiously.

There are introductions, but I don't remember any of their names, just the fact that I need to impress them as well as Mr Diablo.

"Coffee?"

Dad practically snatches the cup from Mr Diablo's assistant's hand. We make small talk about Glasgow, about music news, about future plans.

"So," Enrique Diablo says at last. "Shall we get started?"

My legs are trembling as I head towards the little stage at the far end of the room. One or two more people drift in from the lobby outside the office and loiter at the back of the room, talking in low voices.

He's just Belle in a suit, I tell myself, as the two session musicians discuss the key and the rhythms with Mum before settling themselves down beside me.

"Dance with me," I sing. We worked hard on the rhythm at Spacebar Studios and Dad's old mate Rory got it just right, all sultry and loose. We did so many takes of the song that the beat is still with me, pulsing right beside my heart. These guys

accompanying me have it just right. *"Dance, ooh, dance so close and you will see, flowers twining through the beat, dance with me and feel, oh, feel that heat. . ."* My hands are up by my head, taking on a life of their own as they sway with the rhythm. They do this a lot when I'm really into a song.

"Ain't no time like the present, there ain't a thing out there that doesn't, ooh, doesn't strike the bell and strum the wire, set the world, the world on fire. . ."

My voice fills me up with light. I could float away like a puff of wind.

"Dance, oooh, dance with me."

There is a short silence when the song ends. I don't want to breathe and break the spell.

Enrique Diablo has quiet words with all the other people in the room. There is a lot of nodding.

"There will be caveats, I imagine," he says at last, turning to Mum. "As she is only fifteen."

Mum sits very upright in her chair. "Every caveat you can think of," she says. "She will need to keep up with her schoolwork. She cannot work before seven in the morning or after seven at night. She can put in a maximum of two hours a day during the school week, and no more than four at weekends. When she leaves school, we can adjust the contract, but those are the terms for the present."

He gives a short bark of laughter. "I like your style, Mrs Hall. The tiger looking after her cub. I have no problem with these terms."

I clasp my hands, which have started trembling like crazy. My throat is as dry as the soles of my feet after a day on the beach.

"Does that mean you like me?" I ask, swallowing.

Enrique Diablo steeples his brown fingers together and looks at me with his fierce brown eyes.

"I like you very much, Miss Hall," he says. "Very much indeed. Sound Pacific Records would like to work with you, if that is what you want?"

CHAPTER 14

Sound Pacific want to sign me. It hasn't sunk in yet, to be honest.

"I can't believe he asked if I wanted the deal," I say as Jake and Alex bicker about their favourite dinosaurs in their window seat at our table in the Hard Rock Cafe on Piccadilly. Our starters arrived five minutes ago but we're all so busy talking that no one's touched the food yet. "What was I going to say? 'Uh, no thanks, Mr Diablo, I've had second thoughts'?"

"I liked him," says Mum a bit dreamily. "He had style. And fantastic teeth."

"*I* have style," Dad objects, brushing down his old

plaid shirt, which is covered in breadstick crumbs. "And all my teeth are my own."

"Dad's jealous!" Tina says in a sing-song voice, and Mum and Dad laugh and clink their glasses together.

"Of course we have to get the right deal," Mum says, looking serious again. "I've found a great lawyer who specializes in just these kind of contracts. We'll be safe in his hands, I'm sure. I've set up a meeting for a couple of days' time."

"How long are we staying in London?" Tina asks.

"As long as it takes," Mum replies.

Tina and I exchange grins. The longer it takes, the better!

"My favourite dinosaur was the velociraptor," says Jake.

"The velociraptor was rubbish," Alex scoffs. He has left his cars at the hotel, amazingly, and has a toy stegosaur bought at the museum today instead. The steg has already "eaten" three breadsticks.

"Was not!"

"Was too!"

Even Jake and Alex bickering can't dampen my mood. I feel like someone has just filled me with happy juice, right up to the top. *This is really happening.*

I need to tell Jase.

I grab a handful of garlic bread and get up from the table.

"Back in a sec," I say, waving my phone.

"Send the megastar my love!" Tina calls as I make my way through the restaurant to a quiet corner.

"In your dreams!" I call back, laughing.

I try Jase's mobile first, but can't get through. So I decide to try his hotel instead. I'm about to look it up on my phone when I realize I can't remember what it's called. The Washington? The Accrington? Eek!

I type *MaHunnies Fan Page* into Facebook.

JASE MAHONE
Musician/band

You bring out the Red Devil in me! Jase xx

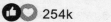 345k   6453 shares

Adriana Wesley

Like this comment if you are a MaHunny!

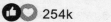 254k

Sadia Kumar

Seeing Jase in concert next wk! Think I'll die of

happyness! #reddeviltour

 1461

Maria Jimenez

I WILL BE 14 TOMORROW JASE SAY HAPPY

BIRTHDAY AND I'LL BE HAPPY FOR EVER!!!!!!

 1603

Come on, I think, feeling a bit overwhelmed by all
the love the fans are pouring over Jase. *Tell me where
he's staying. . .*

Elena Novak

I WILL WAIT FOR YOU 4EVER JASE xxxxx

 3455

Elena Novak has helpfully posted a pic of herself outside the hotel. The message was posted four hours ago. I squint at the screen. BILLINGTON is etched in big gold letters by the shiny glass doors. Gotcha!

I call the Billington right away.

"Hi," I say brightly. "Can I speak to Jase Mahone, please? It's Storm Hall."

"We have no one here by that name, madam."

Yeah, right!

"Look," I say, "it's very important that I speak to him. He knows who I am."

The receptionist repeats the message wearily. I realize she's probably had fans calling all day with stupid reasons why they need to speak to Jase. Hmm. Problem.

"He knows me," I say again. "Really."

"Have you tried his mobile number, madam?"

"Yes, I have," I say. "I can't get through."

I can practically hear the receptionist rolling her eyes. "I'm sorry, madam. Good evening."

"But I—"

She's cut me off. Typical! How am I going to tell Jase my news? Maybe I should Instagram it.

My phone rings as I'm about to give up.

"S'up?" says Jase.

I'm still not used to him calling me like a normal person. I resist the urge to cover my phone with one hand and bellow at the entire restaurant, "I'M ON THE PHONE TO JASE MAHONE!" (It even rhymes.)

"Thank goodness," I say in relief. "I tried you before but I couldn't get through and then I tried the receptionist at your hotel but she was really snotty and I'm really glad you called! I have the most AMAZING news!"

"Storm, can you hold for a sec?"

I hear some mumbling in the background. I'm desperate to tell him about Sound Pacific. Maybe we could celebrate by going somewhere ultra cool together.

"S'up?" he says again after a while. He sounds distracted.

"I've got a record deal!" I say in excitement. "With Sound Pacific! Isn't that the most awesome news you've ever heard?"

There's the muffled burbling again. Why doesn't he say anything? I wait, biting my lip, for him to congratulate me.

"You're kidding," he says. "Sound Pacific? You're not thinking of signing with those dinosaurs, are you?"

Jase doesn't sound impressed. He sounds disappointed. I picture Jake and Alex's toy dinosaurs with a tiny contract on the restaurant table.

"Sound Pacific aren't dinosaurs," I say uncertainly. "They're one of the greatest labels in the world."

"Maybe they were once. But tell me one big act they've signed lately."

I feel like a rabbit in a spotlight. I can't think. Who's that girl, the one everyone's been talking about on Twitter lately? "Lauri B!" I pull the name from somewhere deep in my brain in triumph.

"They signed her last week."

Jase laughs scornfully. "I mean someone *big*, Storm. Not some small-fry kid from Minnesota who hasn't even got a record out yet."

I'm floundering now. This is not how I thought my news would be going down. "They signed Amy Winehouse!" I say.

"That's a looooong time ago, Storm. You can do better than that. Listen, why don't I set up a meeting with my team at Echo?"

"But—"

"Echo is totally down with the youth thing in music right now. Sound Pacific are out of their depth. Seriously, Storm. Let me fix a meeting, OK?"

"Echo are kind of cool, I guess," I say doubtfully, "but all of my heroes recorded with Sound Pacific, so—"

"RecordED, past tense!" Jase interrupts. "You need to sign with a label who's focused on the future, not the past. Talk to Echo, for me. Let me sort a meeting. I'll let you know when I've fixed something up, OK?"

I'm really confused now. But Jase is right at the top of the business, so he must know what he's talking about. I ring off, feeling flatter than a steamrollered flatfish.

Glancing back at the table full of my family, I feel really weird. Sad. Like I can't celebrate any more. There's a little worm niggling in my head now and I can't ignore it.

I Google Echo. Great website, first off. The graphics are slick, the design is street. I scroll through the pictures of the offices. They make Sound Pacific look a little bit . . . I don't know. Old-fashioned? Ooh, they have one of Jase's videos on their site! Clicking on it, I lose my train of thought for a while and admire his abs.

I hit speed dial for my BF.

"I don't know what to do," I blurt. And I tell her all about Sound Pacific and Jase and Echo.

"Rewind, Storm," says Belle when I've run out of breath. "Sound Pacific want to sign you? That's incredible!"

I get a little whiff of happiness back in my brain.

"It was so amazing, Belle," I say, remembering the delicious moment it happened. "Enrique Diablo was so nice and kind and I really nailed the song."

"That's fantastic; I'd bite their hand off if I were you. But now Jase is suggesting his label? Coco Music?"

"Echo," I correct. "They haven't been going as long as Sound Pacific but Jase says they're really edgy and signing all these great young acts at the moment."

"Jase says?"

Belle's voice has a sudden edge to it that I don't like.

"Music is his business, Belle," I point out. "He wouldn't give me bad advice."

"Nor would I!"

"I know you wouldn't, but you don't know anything about the music business, so I have to listen to Jase, OK?"

"Listen to him?" Belle checks. "Or do what he says? Jase Mahone isn't the only person with an opinion worth hearing, Storm. What do your parents think?"

I think of Mum, and how excited she is about the Sound Pacific deal. I squirm a bit and decide to change the subject.

"How's Colin?"

"He's great," says Belle after a moment. "He's helping me with the party right now. I know there's still a couple of weeks to go, but there's still loads to plan."

"We've been planning your sixteenth birthday party since we were nine," I remind her. "How much more work do you need to do?"

"Those plans we made need a little revising," Belle says, and I can hear a grin in her voice. "Somehow I don't think we're going to get 1D to play, however many cookies we spend."

"I remember those birthday plans like we made them yesterday," I tell her. "You were going to have a space-age theme while I was going for the full chocolate experience."

"You even wanted Hot Chocolate to play!"

"Imagine if you really could pay people and buy

stuff with cookies," I say fondly. "The world would be a better place."

Belle snorts with agreement. "I showed Colin our old plans the other day," she says. "He thinks the cookie thing is hilarious. He asks after you a lot, you know."

I feel a little thrill in my stomach. "He does?"

"He wants to know if you'll remember us when you get famous."

"Of course I will!" I say. Like she has to ask!

"He's so lovely, Storm," says Belle. "He took me to the planetarium because I told him about the theme for my party. . ."

If I signed with Echo, I think as Belle rambles on, I could see Jase all the time. We'd go on joint promotional tours; maybe we'd even do a duet. The papers would go mad for us. Sound Pacific wouldn't be able to arrange that as neatly as Echo could. It would be—

". . . and then we landed back on Earth in our spaceship with lots of free alien chocolate bars," Belle says.

"Nice," I say absently.

Belle sighs. "When are you going to learn that you need to listen as well as talk to your friends, Storm?" she says. "See you around."

"I—"

But she's already hung up. What was she talking about anyway? Alien chocolates?

Ping.

My producer Adrian is stoked about meeting you. Come to a party with me tonight and I'll introduce you!

Jase xx

CHAPTER 15

"Storm! Jase! This way! Over here!"

I'm blinking at the flashes but Jase is with me so that's OK.

"Stick with me," he whispers in my ear, slinging his arm round my neck to pull me close. He smells lovely, all fresh and grassy. The cameras flash harder. This feels like I'm in the middle of a crazy lightning storm. "You're doing great."

I stumble slightly on my new (and totally incredible) shoes. They are platforms in a rainbow of colours with laces that go up to my knees. And I smile and I wave and I wave and I smile and I try not to fall over my own feet because that would be the most embarrassing thing in the world.

"Have you been seeing each other for long, Jase?"

"How does Kendall feel about it?"

"She's cool," says Jase. "We're still good friends."

I can't really be with a guy whose most recent ex is Kendall Jenner, can I? That's just insane. All of this – everything in the past few days – has been totally insane. There have been parties every night, sometimes two or three, one after the other. Jase gets me through the door every time, makes sure that we're photographed together, bigs me up at every opportunity. I'm so lucky that he's taken me under his wing. This world is even bigger and crazier than I realized.

"Are you signing with Echo Music, Storm?"

There's only been questions for Jase so far, so having a question directed at me catches me out. I gape like a fish and wonder what to say. I haven't spoken to Mum and Dad about Jase's idea yet. Every party we go to, Jase says his producer will be there, but I haven't met him yet so the Sound

Pacific deal is still in negotiation. Am I going to sign with Echo or not?

"Never say never!" Jase says, winking at the cameras. "Thanks, coming through. . . Hey, Harry! Bring us some drinks, will you?"

"You got it, Jase!"

The boy-band sensation second only in famosity to Jase threads his way back towards us, balancing three drinks in his hands.

"Good to meet you at last, Storm," he says, and clinks glasses with me.

It's all I can do not to throw my drink all over him and scream. How am I here? How has this happened to me, a wee Glasgow girl?

"Let's dance," says Jase.

I've hardly got my lips to my drink before Jase is dragging me to the dance floor. He pulls me towards him, grinning. My legs still don't feel as if they're functioning properly yet. We start dancing, and I begin to relax.

"This is an incredible party!" I shout at Jase as we swing around under the glitter ball above our heads.

"Yeah ... I guess so," says Jase. "But the party bags at this place are always awesome. Are you dancing, Harry?"

I snap a few pics of me and Harry and Jase all whirling around the floor together. No one will ever believe me if I don't get the photographic evidence.

Storm Hall @stormhall_official
Jase dances like a Red Devil and Harry fetched me a drink. #justsayin #parteee ☺

I'm about to take another pic back at the bar when my phone rings.

"We're outside, Storm, love," says Mum. "We said eleven, if you remember?"

I look furtively at Jase and Harry, who are propping up the bar beside me. I don't want them to think I'm a kid because I'm talking to my mum mid-party. They're talking magazine covers.

"So I did *Wonderland* in this suit made of feathers, man they made me sneeze. . ."

"I didn't get Miley's look for *i-D*, what was she thinking. . ."

I think I'm safe for a bit. "We only just got here, Mum," I begin in my most persuasive voice. "It's an incredible party, the drinks are free and the music is hot and you'll never guess what! Harry—"

"You're not drinking, are you?" Mum interrupts. "You are only fifteen. Please don't keep us waiting, love, people keep trying to steal our taxi."

"But—"

"Now, Storm! We have a meeting with Leo first thing to sort out the finer details of your contract with Sound Pacific."

I bet Jase and Harry's mums don't show up at parties and drag them home, I think. Reluctantly I try to get Jase's attention.

"I have to go," I begin, but Jase sees someone over my head and he waves and yells: "Adrian! At last! Come meet my new friend!"

A very tall, very thin man with bleached-blond buzz cut and a ring through his nose throws his arms round me. Thank goodness I'm leaning against the bar because there's no way the shoes would have withstood the impact by themselves.

"Hi," I say as this Adrian guy holds me at arm's length and beams at me like he's known me for ever. "You're Jase's producer, right?"

"Jase, she's gorgeous," gasps Adrian. "Such a fierce look. Check out the hair. And darling girl, wherever did you get those shoes? They are divine."

I open my mouth to tell him but he's already ploughing on.

"I had no idea you were so pretty," he says. "Turn around, darling."

I do as he suggests, feeling a little bit foolish.

"Jase, she has *so* much potential. Baby girl, we have to fix a meeting at the office. Can you do that for me?"

He's tweaking my hair, adjusting the curl over my ear. It's a bit intense.

I glance at Jase for reassurance. He smiles right back at me, nodding.

"Sure," I say, trying not to think about what Mum would say about this guy. "So, you've heard my music?"

"She's so great," Jase says, draping his arm protectively around my neck. "I played you her stuff, right?"

"Sure you did." Adrian is still eating me up with his eyes. "But honey, with a look like this, you don't have to open your mouth and sing another note. You are just charming."

"But I *want* to sing," I say in surprise.

"Course you do. I'm just messing with you. I'll call you, OK?"

He looks me over one more time, nods to himself and sways away through the crowd.

"He's really cool," says Jase. "Totally loved the song I played him."

I relax a bit. "Which song was it?"

"Can't remember right now." Jase's eyes wander over my right shoulder. "Hey, Mila, baby! I didn't know you were in town!"

My phone rings.

"Sorry," I say, tearing my eyes from Mila's famous dark gaze. "I just have to take this. . ."

"We're still waiting, Storm." Mum sounds impatient on the other end of the phone. "Do you want me to come in there and drag you out?"

I shrivel inside at the thought of Jase and Mila and Harry and all these famous, cool people seeing me being fetched out of the party by my *mother*.

"I'm coming," I say, backing away from Jase and Mila with an apologetic wave. I don't know what to think of Adrian from Echo Music. I don't know what to think about my life right now, period. "I'll be out in a minute, Mum. Don't come in. Promise me you won't come in?"

As I am slipping my phone back into my clutch I see that I've missed two calls from Belle. *She would go crazy for this place*, I think, gazing at the beautiful people and the glittering interior of the club. She would go utterly nuts. I will call her in the morning.

"Sneaking off, huh? Without saying goodbye?"

Jase catches me as I'm almost at the doors. He wraps his arms round my waist and rests his forehead against mine, smiling into my eyes. I melt like ice cream on a hot car bonnet.

"I have to go," I tell him. "Mum and Dad are waiting outside." And I roll my eyes to convey exactly how much of a drag being fifteen can be.

"Baby," Jase says, pulling me against his warm body. "Adrian thinks you're incredible. When you sign with us, we're going to have such good times."

I gaze into his eyes. I'm feeling a little hypnotized, if I'm honest.

"Miss you already," Jase whispers.

And he kisses me. Right on the lips.

CHAPTER 16

Tina doesn't believe that it happened. I don't believe it happened either, except that I was there, being kissed.

"Why would Jase Mahone kiss a stinker like you?"

"Because he likes me," I reply dreamily. I realize how tired I am the minute I flop down on the bed in my and Tina's hotel room. My feet hurt but I don't care. In my head, I'm walking on clouds.

Tina snorts. "Nice Photoshopping on Instagram, by the way," she adds. "You and Jase and Harry Styles. As if."

And the next thing I know it's morning and I *still* can't get Tina to believe the truth, even over croissants and orange juice in the hotel restaurant. Until Mum brings the papers to our table.

The photographer caught the exact moment when Jase kissed me. We're in this halo of party light and the shoes look incredible. We're in every paper, and headline news in half of them.

STORMY WEATHER!

TEEN HEART-THROB
STRUCK BY LIGHTNING!

JASE KICKS
UP A STORM!

"I'm *trying* to eat my breakfast here," says Tina, pushing the paper away as Jake and Alex scream with laughter.

"I hope that's all he did," says Mum.

I flush with embarrassment. "Mum! It was just a

kiss. I was outside with you about twenty seconds after it happened!"

Mum tuts. "Still. How old is he?"

"Oh, sixteen, I think," I lie. He's seventeen.

"Well, you're only fifteen."

I put on my most surprised face. "Am I?" I say. "I had no idea."

"That's enough lip, thank you, Storm," says Mum sharply.

There's a cluster of reporters on the steps outside the hotel. I'm guessing they read the papers too. Thank goodness I am wearing a great outfit, with shades that are almost the size of my head. The camera flashes are intense.

"How long have you been dating Jase, Storm?"

"Are you guys going to collaborate?"

"I hear you're signing with Sound Pacific?"

I want to stop and chat, but Mum pushes me through the crowd and practically throws me into our waiting taxi. Even as we're driving off, the paps are chasing after us. I wave at them through the back window.

"This is all too much," says Mum, dusting down her jacket. "The press attention feels very inappropriate. You're only—"

"Fifteen," I say through gritted teeth. "Believe me, Mum, I KNOW."

The being-fifteen thing winds me up the whole way to Leo Greenwood's office. I've heard it a hundred times in just a couple of days. Maybe Echo could do something in my contract that would treat me like an adult. I'm entering a proper career, aren't I? That ought to count for SOMETHING in the maturity stakes. I spend at least half of the journey in a state of grouchiness. The rest of the time I imagine me and Jase in a recording studio together. We would be recording our mega-million-selling album and kissing in between and the sound engineers would tell us off and we wouldn't care. I have to sign with Echo. I HAVE to.

"Well, now," says Leo Greenwood in amusement. "I like a girl who knows how to make a name for herself."

My new lawyer is handsome in an old silver fox

kind of way, with sharp dark eyes that feel as if they can see right into my soul.

"Mr Greenwood," says Mum, shaking his hand vigorously. "Thank you so much for seeing us."

"My pleasure, believe me," says Leo. "You have a great voice, Storm. I know that you'll do well with Sound Pacific."

My stomach flips nervously. The more I think about it, the less I want to work with Sound Pacific. Enrique Diablo may be brilliant at what he does, but he's *ancient*. He worked with the *Beatles*. Everything about Echo seems so much cooler, brighter, edgier. What if I'm making a huge mistake?

Leo Greenwood's office is totally unlike Enrique Diablo's, with old wooden panelling, stacks of paper everywhere and walls lined with LPs. He's like me, I realize, as I trail through the albums. Most of his records are Sound Pacific. Something soulful and funky is playing quietly on the sleek music system in one corner of the office. I pick up the album cover beside the system. It's a moody shot of the band, just the kind of photography I love – all shadow and suggestion. Even the band name is cool: they're called the Brink.

"Do you like them?" the lawyer asks me as Mum sits down.

"Who are they?" I ask.

"Clients of mine. With a sound that gets right into your boots."

I nod. I know what he means.

"You have a similar sound," he says.

I flush with pleasure. "You've heard my music?"

"I make a point of listening to the talent I work with," he says with a grin. "Shall we get down to business? We've sorted out most of the details with Sound Pacific, but there are one or two snags that we need to talk about."

I browse on through his records as he and Mum discuss the dusty details of the contract, running my fingers over the narrow LP spines, humming along to the track on the stereo. I wish I felt as comfortable about the Sound Pacific deal as I do about being in this office. Every album I lift from the collection is another famous, old name. Every single one has

Sound Pacific's wavy logo on the back. Apart from the Brink (who I notice are signed to a different label) where is the new music, the latest sale-busting name?

"Everything OK?"

I stop running my fingers along the LPs. "Are you sure I'm doing the right thing, Mr Greenwood?" I ask nervously. "Signing with Sound Pacific?"

"They're a great label," he says. "Solid, well respected. What's not to like? And please, call me Leo."

Mum looks alarmed. "You're not changing your mind, are you, Storm?"

Talk about putting me on the defensive.

"What if I am?" I say. "I was thinking about Echo, actually. Maybe they would suit me better, you know?"

"Echo?" Mum looks appalled. "They're gimmicky and flashy. They don't do your kind of music at all."

I should know what my kind of music is, I think.

"I'm allowed to *think* about them," I say crossly.

"This is my career, Mum. There's no need to get so mad."

"Storm, we're three-quarters of the way through a very delicate negotiation! You are extremely lucky that Sound Pacific are interested. Do you know how many kids your age would give their souls for a chance like this?"

There she goes again. Going on about what a kid I am. And anyway, it's talent that's got me this far, isn't it? Not luck.

"Why is it always about my age?" I demand. "This is my *life*, Mum!"

"It's tough being young," says Leo. His face is genuinely sympathetic, and I give him a grateful smile.

Mum mutters something under her breath. "I'm sorry, Leo," she says. "I'm sure it's just nerves that are making Storm behave this way. We're sure we're doing the right thing for her career."

I sit silently for the rest of the meeting, occasionally picking at my nails and resisting the urge to play with my phone. Although I'm desperate to catch up with what's online, Leo is too nice for that kind of rudeness.

"Great," Mum concludes after another forty minutes. "I think this is looking watertight now. Let us know how Sound Pacific react to those new clauses, Leo, and we'll take it from there. OK?"

We all shake hands. Leo puts his other hand on top of mine as he shakes it.

"Call me any time, Storm," he says, looking intently into my eyes. I really think he means it.

I take out my phone the minute we climb into the taxi.

"What was that about in there, Storm?" Mum asks. "Aren't you pleased about the deal with Sound Pacific?"

I shrug as non-committally as I can. She looks at me and sighs.

"Well," she says, "we're in safe hands with Leo at least. Whatever happens next."

Jase and I are all over the net. I scroll down page after page, marvelling at the way a photo can go from place to place in the blink of an eye. We're

trending on Twitter. The photo I took of me and Jase
and the Boy Band Famosity has been shared over ten
thousand times. It makes me feel giddy.

Ping.

> Call me soon Storm, OK? We need to talk about
> the party!
> Belle xx

Belle has read the papers today, then. I grin and
reply.

> It was incredible! And everything you've read
> about it is true!!! #jase #kiss
> xxx

Ping.

> Can U get away this pm? Adrian wants to see
> you in the Echo offices. Jase xx
> PS You look so great in that pic, I want to kiss
> you all over again!

My heart skips a beat.

"Do we, uh, have any plans this afternoon?" I ask Mum as the taxi pulls into the hotel parking bay. "I think I need to rest."

"I was thinking we'd take Tina shopping to make up for all the time she's spending with the boys," says Mum. "But you're right, you ought to rest, Storm. Partying every night can really take it out of you when you're fifteen."

I ride that one with hardly a blink. "Yes," I say. "Sounds good."

Needless to say, resting isn't at the top of my list of Things to Do this afternoon.

It's time for me to make a few decisions of my own.

CHAPTER 17

"Sleep well, Storm," says Mum at the door to the suite. "We'll see you in a few hours."

I yawn obediently. "Where's Dad?"

"He's taken the boys back to the Natural History Museum. Alex wants another dinosaur."

"Are you coming, Mum?" Tina calls from the hallway.

I hear my sister excitedly instructing Mum exactly where she wants to go this afternoon ("First it has to be Topshop, but then maybe Niketown, or maybe we could do Niketown first – they're next to each other, I think...") until their voices fade to nothing. I lie still for about five minutes, wondering nervously about what I'm going to do.

I'm just going to listen to what Echo has to say, I reason with myself as – coast clear – I pick out my most outrageous outfit for the afternoon. Orange jacket, mesh tee, bondage trousers, spike heels. Perfect. It's a look that says, I know my own mind. I'm not a kid, and I can make mature decisions all by myself. It's also a look that I know Jase will freak for. He already told me how much he likes this jacket.

I take extra care with my make-up. Too much and I'll look like I'm trying too hard. Too little and I'll undo all the good grown-up work my outfit is doing for me. Hair just so. Extra dab of electric-blue eyeliner: killer.

"Come get me, paps," I tell my reflection, pouting a few times to get my expression right and snapping off a couple of selfies to keep my followers happy. I pick up my bag and tiptoe out of the room. Halfway to the lift, I remember that I don't have to tiptoe anywhere. I'm free! I'm going to see Jase, and no one can stop me!

"You might want to go out the back, Miss Hall," offers the receptionist as I stride as confidently as I can through the main hall. "There are a lot of photographers out there today."

I smile at her. "That's half the fun," I say, and I wink before I drop my sunglasses on to my nose.

The cameras are flashing almost before I've reached the top step.

"Storm! This way! I love your hair! I love your outfit!"

I smile and pose for a few seconds, relishing the fact that I'm doing this my own way for once. After a while though, it gets a little much. I try to make my way to the kerb to hail a taxi. It's harder than I thought it would be.

A girl barges me as I reach for the handle of the cab.

"Jase is *mine*! You might have kissed him but that changes nothing. Stay away from him."

It's the girl who posted a pic of herself outside Jase's hotel the other day. She's wearing a Red Devil tee and there's a love heart biro-ed on her neck.

They're biro-ed all the way up her arms too, with Jase's name squeezed into all the remaining spaces. I feel nervous as I pull at the cab door. I've heard that Jase's fangirls can be a bit weird.

"Stay away!" she screams at me through the cab window as the cabbie pulls away.

"Where to, love?" says the cabbie.

My heart is pounding uncomfortably in my chest. It takes me a minute to realize he's waiting for a reply.

"Echo Music, Borough High Street," I say, swallowing. "As fast as you can, please."

I'm still a bit shaky when I reach the gleaming glass towers of Echo Music. Checking a little fearfully out of the window before I get out, I only just remember to pay the cabbie before I'm scooting through the doors and rushing up to the reception desk. My sunglasses are sliding around on my sweaty nose like a toddler on a skating rink.

"Yes?"

"Storm Hall," I say. I cast a glance over my

shoulder, half expecting Biro Girl to be right behind me. "To see Adrian . . . um. . ."

I realize I don't know Jase's producer's surname. But I'm saved from the receptionist's next question by a shout from the lift.

"I saw you arrive in the taxi, baby girl!" says Adrian, gliding towards me with his arms outstretched. "You are looking so hot, honey! Unbelievable outfit! Come with me, come, come!"

As we glide up in the lift, he strokes the fringed epaulettes on my shoulders like you might stroke a cat. "Gorgeous," he murmurs. "So hot. Jase is totally right about you. Your look will take you far."

I smile weakly. Too many compliments at once does my head in. "Is Jase here?" I ask.

"Of course he's here," Adrian says, ushering me out of the lift into a virtually silent corridor lined with neon-bright artwork. "He cannot wait to see you, baby. You two are the talk of the town."

Adrian's office is smaller than I was expecting,

and a little dark. My stomach flips to see Jase standing in silhouette by the window.

"You changed your hair!" I blurt.

Jase rubs his hand over the reddish buzz cut that now sits on top of his head. "Adrian says my look was getting a little tired," he says. "Pretty good, huh?"

I go to him and he hugs me briefly. I feel a pang for his blond locks. The red is striking, but it doesn't suit him quite as well.

"My jacket clashes with you," I joke.

Jase looks serious. "Can you take it off?" he asks.

Surprised, I do as I'm told, even though I'd worn it specially. He relaxes and hugs me again.

"We look so great together, don't we?" he says, rubbing his finger down my cheek. "We should take a picture to mark the occasion."

I hadn't planned on taking off the jacket. My tee has a little stain on the front which you can't see when the jacket is on, but which now feels as big as a house. I hold my arm awkwardly across my front and smile for Jase's picture. Adrian is watching us, glancing from Jase to me and back again.

"It's so great that you want to sign with us, honey," he says. "You guys look so gorgeous together."

"Oh, I'm just here to talk," I begin, but Adrian has clicked his fingers and already the room has three more people in it.

"It's a standard contract," Adrian says, smiling at me. "Nothing tricky about it. No need for lawyers. They slow things down, don't you find?"

I picture Leo Greenwood in his wood-panelled office, his music burbling around him. I open my mouth.

"Of course you do," says Adrian briskly before I say anything else. "Everyone hates lawyers in our business. Jase outlined everything for you, yes?"

"I've told her what a great label Echo is," Jase says. He squeezes me warmly round the shoulders. "And all the incredible things you can do for Storm's career."

I try to remember what Jase has told me. Not much, if I'm honest. But he's has done OK with Echo, hasn't he? More than OK.

"Do you want me to sing?" I ask, remembering how they had done it at Sound Pacific.

"Baby, we'd LOVE you to sing!" Adrian exclaims.

The thought of singing makes me relax a little more into myself. I look around for a microphone. I nailed "Dance with Me" for Sound Pacific, there's no reason why I can't nail it even better for—

"Only unfortunately we have no session musicians available to accompany you today," Adrian continues. He makes a sad face. "So the exciting part will have to wait. But we know you're right for us. You're so fresh and exciting, honey. I've only just met you, but already I can't get enough of what I'm seeing."

Jase rubs my shoulder. "You're doing great," he says, looking into my eyes.

"This is the right thing to do, isn't it?" I ask him, suddenly feeling anxious.

Jase takes one of my curls and winds it round his finger. He gives it a gentle tug. "You're a strong person, Storm," he says. "Don't tell me you can't make your own decisions?"

My resolve hardens. *Jase and I could really have a musical future together,* I think as I pick up the pen Adrian has passed towards me. Echo Music is the right place for us both. Together, the world is going to be ours.

CHAPTER 18

Celebrity News @celebnewsstories

Whispers on the wind that @stormhall_official

signed w/ @EchoMusicLtd despite rumour that

@SoundPacific snapped that prize?

News 4 Yous @news4youz

BREAKING NEWS @jasemreal's girl

@stormhall_official deal w/ @EchoMusicLtd

OFFICIAL. Revenge for Lauri B,

@SoundPacific?

Jase Fan Gurl AAA @marrymejase

.@jasem4real tell me U & @stormhall_official

not true #love #passion #mahunny PS pls follow
me

Jase Mahone @jasem4real
Congratulations @stormhall_official and
welcome to the @EchoMusicLtd family! #style
#reddevil #music

News 4 Youz @news4youz
.@SoundPacific rumoured to be seeking lawsuit
v @stormhall_official for calling them dinosaurs
#heardithere1st

"I can't believe you called Sound Pacific
dinosaurs," Tina remarks over her bowl of muesli.

We are trapped in our hotel room with room
service breakfast because Dad thinks it's the safest
thing to do. I think he's right. Every time I twitch
the curtains, there seem to be more paps outside,
clambering over each other for a glimpse whenever
someone tries to leave the hotel.

"I didn't," I insist. I can hardly tear my eyes from

my Twitter feed. Signing with Echo was supposed to be something to celebrate, but no one seems to be happy for me, not online or IRL or *anywhere*. Except Jase, of course. Thank goodness for him.

"Even if you didn't," Tina says with a smirk, "it's out there now so that's what people are going to think."

I swear I never called Sound Pacific dinosaurs. But my brain is so fried by all this chaos that maybe I did. I scroll cautiously back through my feed, pause and groan.

Storm Hall @stormhall_official
Watch out dinosaurs!!! @SoundPacific @jasem4real

"We were passing the Natural History Museum! I took a photo!" I rub my aching head. "They can't sue me for that, can they?"

Mum stalks into the room, phone pressed to her head. She laser-deaths me with her eyes.

"Leo, hello, Meggie Hall here... Yes... Yes, all

true, apparently. . . I'm so sorry, we had no idea she was planning on doing this. . ."

I do feel bad about Leo. He was lovely to me, and he, Mum and Dad did loads of work on the Sound Pacific contract. But I've done the right thing. Echo Music is Jase's label, I remind myself, and he's a megastar for a reason. I want to be a megastar too. What's wrong with that?

"I'm so embarrassed," says Mum, putting her phone down on the table so hard that I worry she cracked the screen.

I prepare myself for the tidal wave. When it comes – oh boy. It comes.

"Your father and I have put so much work into this for you, Storm! How could you let us down? How could you sneak out and lie and sign your name on a contract without telling us? It's so careless! Echo Music won't look after you; they don't even produce your kind of music! Oh, *what* is Enrique Diablo going to say?"

"Something in Spanish, probably," says Tina. "And it won't be good."

My sister's enjoying this. I decide it's time to stand up for myself.

"You were making all the decisions!" I say. "It was time for me to make a decision of my own. You knew I was having second thoughts, I even said so in that meeting with Leo, but you just told me off!"

"You're a VERY silly girl," Mum says.

"You're always on at me about being a girl, being fifteen, being a kid," I say furiously. "Well, I have a newsflash. I'm not a kid any more!"

I stalk out of our living room and into my and Tina's bedroom. There's nowhere else to go from here except our en suite bathroom or the walk-in wardrobe, so I just shut the door and lean against it and close my eyes and hope that all of this will go away very soon. Then I get on my hands and knees and crawl under the bed, clutching my phone tightly to my chest.

My phone rings.

"Jase?" I say hopefully, pressing the phone to my ear and staring at the underside of my hotel bed.

"Nope."

I can tell already from the tone of Belle's voice that she's mad at me too.

"What do you think you're doing, you idiot?"

"Firstly," I say, "I'm not an idiot."

"Secondly, you ARE," Belle says bluntly. "Echo is good, but they're young and they aren't right for your sound or your music. Sound Pacific is a much better fit for you."

Tears prick hotly in my eyes. "I know what fits me, thanks very much."

"Tell me one artist represented by Echo that you like. You know, apart from loverboy."

"Loads of people, OK?" I say defensively. "People you've probably never heard of because they are too cool."

Belle snorts at that. "Jase put you up to this, didn't he?"

"No one put me up to anything!"

"I bet he fixed the whole thing. He's using you to big up his own profile. And you're a lot stupider than I thought if you can't see that."

I can't believe Belle is being so nasty to me. I hit back with the only weapon I've got.

"Last time I looked, I'm the one with a singing contract around here, Belle, not you."

"That's low, even for you," Belle says in disgust. Her tone makes me wish I hadn't said it (even though it's true). "Look, if you want to dig yourself a lovely big hole and bury yourself in it, go right ahead. I can't be bothered to pull you out any more."

The dial tone buzzes in my head like an angry wasp.

Why can't anyone be happy for me? Is it too much to ask?

I wriggle out from under the bed and listen at the bedroom door. Everyone's gone off without me. Fine. If they don't want my company, then I don't want theirs either.

I pull on the first clothes I can find. Then the second clothes, then the third and the fourth until I've got the shoe/jacket combo right. Then I fix my make-up and grab a pair of sunglasses (large and pink and awesome), pick up my bag and head out of the hotel room. I'm sick of hiding and I'm not scared. I'm going to face my public and everything's going to be fine.

Twenty-five minutes later, I'm hiding in a bush. It smells of dog wee with a dollop of fear. I curl my arms round my knees, feel my toes tingle with a lack of circulation and wish I hadn't chosen such a tight pair of trousers.

Feet pound past, and there are shouts.

"Are you and Jase going to get married?"

"They say Sound Pacific are going to sue you, can you comment?"

"Has Echo signed you in revenge for Sound Pacific poaching Lauri B, Storm?"

"Leave Jase alone! He's mine!"

I started running almost from the moment I got out of the hotel and the fangirl with the biro-ed hearts on her arms got in my face and started shouting at me while the paps went insane. Someone kicked me. Someone else trod on my toe. I tried to answer their questions but everything got loud and confusing and all I could think of was Mum's fury and Enrique Diablo's wrinkly face and how upset Leo must have been by the news that all their work on the Sound Pacific contract had been for nothing and I panicked. And now I'm in this stinky bush and I've got no idea where I am or where the hotel is or anything.

I cautiously dial Belle's number.

"Pick up, pick up," I mumble under my breath.

She doesn't. I try Jase next.

"S'up?"

I sag with relief. "Oh, thank goodness, it's me, Storm, and I need your help, I'm in a bush—"

"—through to my voicemail. Leave a message so my people can call your people. Gotta fly!"

I hang up before the beeps. Who else can I call? Mum's too mad, Tina's too annoying, Dad dropped his phone in a full mug of finest Colombian roast this morning when I told everyone about Echo. I bury my head against my knees again and try my very best to *think*. It's hard and feels weird, like the cogs need oiling or something. It's clear I haven't been doing much thinking lately.

A little brown bird hops past as I'm racking my brains for a plan. She's so small and boring that I hardly notice her until the last minute. When I do, she gives me an idea.

I take off my bright blue jacket and my heavy gold belt and my pink sunnies and tuck them into the hedge for some lucky passer-by to find. I reluctantly peel my electric-blue heels off my feet and tuck them into the hedge as well. I find an old elastic band in the bottom of my bag, so I plait my hair tightly and tie the elastic round the end. Last of all I turn my bag inside out so the gold bits are on the inside the grey printed lining. Then I uncurl from the hedge, shriek and hop up and down for a bit while the circulation returns to my legs, and set off in what I hope is the right direction. The pavement is cold under my bare feet.

At the first souvenir shop I pass, I grab a large black sweatshirt with MY DAD WENT TO LONDON AND ALL I GOT WAS THIS LOUSY HOODIE on it, a cheap pair of sunglasses and some Union Jack flip-flops. No one looks at me as I pay for my purchases. No one stares as I study a map on a nearby bus stop and work out where the hotel is. I keep my eyes down as I scurry along the road, feeling the dirt of London seeping between my toes. I almost cry with relief when I glimpse the big white front of our hotel.

I have the Echo deal, I have the Echo deal, I tell myself, limping slightly as I hurry towards the hotel doors. At least no one can take THAT away from me.

CHAPTER 19

"You won't even have your Echo deal if you don't hurry up, Storm," Mum says.

"I'll just be a minute," I tell her, frantically applying blue mascara. Too much? Too little? I'm trying to remember all the things that Adrian liked about my look when we met and recreate them for this morning's meeting. We're heading for the Echo office to discuss "the finer details" of my deal. My stomach feels as if it's full of goldfish swimming around and looking for an exit.

"Isn't this exciting?" Dad says as we climb into our waiting taxi. We're round the back of the hotel, for obvious reasons. Tina and the boys went out the front about half an hour ago, headed for Madame Tussauds.

"Do be quiet, Bernie," Mum snaps. "Leo can't meet us at the Echo offices this morning, so we're on our own. I wish Echo had been more flexible about the meeting time."

"So," says Dad ten minutes into the taxi ride. "Which songs did you sing for this Adrian guy that made him love you so much, Storm?"

I stop chewing the side of my thumb. "I didn't sing any," I say.

"They signed you without hearing your voice?"

The goldfish swim faster.

"Jase played them one of my songs," I say a bit defiantly. "That's how Adrian knew he liked me."

"Which song?"

"I don't know." I know how stupid it sounds the moment I say it.

"Hmm," says Mum.

"I've been listening to some of Echo's bands, Storm," says Dad. "They all have a very ... professional sound."

I look at him for reassurance. "That's good, right?'

"Yes, yes," Dad soothes. "With their great sound engineering and your old dad's magic mixing ear and your mother managing us with her usual blend of power and wisdom, we're all going to be the best of friends."

We reach Echo twenty minutes later, where the girl in the black leather skirt is waiting for us in reception. A huge, illuminated image of Jase's Red Devil tour hangs on the wall beside a heavy steel clock, which reads ten to ten.

"Mr Barry will see you in the conference room," Leather Skirt says. "He's running late but he'll be here as soon as he can."

Mum narrows her eyes. "How late?"

The receptionist smiles. "Help yourselves to coffee," she says.

We sit in the huge Echo reception area on uncomfortable white sofas. Mum watches the ticking clock the way a dog might watch an empty food bowl. Dad drinks so much coffee from the automatic vending machine that he keeps excusing himself and vanishing to the loo. I scroll endlessly through my phone, text Jase, text Belle, then delete the text before I send it because I don't know what to say, text Jase again, update a few social profiles with pics of the Echo reception area and a few upbeat phrases like "Start of the rest of my life!" and "Dream big and make it happen!" I can't bring myself to take a selfie. I'm too nervous.

At twenty past eleven, Leather Skirt takes a call at the desk and beckons us over.

"About time," Mum says loudly. I blush and squirm and wish I was somewhere else.

"I'm sorry," says Leather Skirt, holding up one red-taloned hand at Dad. "Would you mind waiting out here, Mr Hall?"

Dad pauses halfway out of the sofa.

"My husband is with us," says Mum.

"He mixes all my music, he needs to be at the meeting," I add.

Leather Skirt smiles coolly. "I'm sorry."

"This is nonsense," Mum says briskly. "My husband will join us. Come along, Bernie."

"What seems to be the trouble?" says a voice as Leather Skirt and Mum lock battle gazes.

It's Adrian. He's taller than I remember, and less smiley.

"I want my dad at the meeting," I say. For once, I don't care how young I sound.

Adrian's eyes brighten when he sees me. "Angel! You are looking sensational today, truly. And all this without a stylist?"

"My father," I repeat. "He needs to be at the—"

Adrian has switched his gaze to Mum. "So sorry I'm late, quite beyond my control. We only have about twenty minutes to talk, so shall we press on?"

He tries to usher me and Mum down the corridor ahead of him, one in each arm. Dad hovers by the sofas uncertainly.

"Mr Barry," Mum says in a tone of voice I haven't heard since Jake and Alex crayoned rude words all over the living-room wall. "We are going nowhere without my husband."

"We only deal with the talent and the manager."

"He is a part of the 'talent', as you put it," Mum insists.

Adrian looks at Dad's T-shirt/suit combo. "I'm sure he's very good at mixing amateur tracks," he says, "but we have a specialist team to do that for us. No no, he will have to leave."

"If he leaves, so do we," says Mum.

I say the same thing, at exactly the same time.

"Impossible, I'm afraid," says Adrian. "We have a signed and witnessed contract stating that this little treasure is legally obliged to do things our way. Come along now."

Somehow Mum and I find ourselves in the conference room without Dad. Four other people are there. I recognize two of them from last night as Echo's lawyers. The other two look like a pair of peacocks, with brightly coloured hair and make-up. Mum takes the contract Adrian is extending to her and reads it as the Peacocks grab me and literally spin me round on my feet.

"Adorable! But too much hair, of course," says

Peacock One. "When it's in anything less than peak condition, long hair can be so ageing."

"The skin is poor," says Peacock Two as he turns my chin from side to side. "But nothing a peel won't cure."

"With a bit of work, we could have another Jinxxy on our hands," says Peacock One.

The Peacocks start singing the song that's everywhere at the moment. It's irritating enough on the radio, let alone when it's being sung right in your face.

"*I'm so pretty, a real little fittie, won't you take me dancing in New York City...*" Peacock One is even doing the dance, the one that's been a craze in school playgrounds lately with all the kids whirling and grinding to the poppy beat. Jinxxy must be on the Echo label.

Mum sinks into a chair and places the contract on the tabletop. "We can't agree to all of this," she says.

"We have a contract, Mrs Hall," says Adrian. "And we're going to make your daughter a superstar. Trust me."

The rest of the meeting is brief. I relax only when Mum and I get a tour of the in-house studio and Adrian starts talking about recording sessions. This kind of language, I get. It will be weird not having Dad on the mixing desk, but I suppose I'll have to suck it up if I'm going to be professional about this.

At the end of the meeting, I head for the bathroom. The poster of Jase from reception is on the back of the cubicle door. I stare at his handsome face pre-buzz cut and try to relax. The Jinxxy song may be annoying but it's successful. These guys know what they're doing.

I call Jase's number. I really need to see him. Maybe we can go out tonight.

He picks up after an agonizing ten rings.

"Baby! How's it going?"

I think about Echo's state-of-the-art recording studio, how soon all these fussy details will be over and it'll be back to me and the music. "OK, I think," I say. "These two weirdly dressed guys are talking about cutting my hair though."

"That's Eric and Derek. Total style geniuses.

They fixed my new look last week and sales are soaring. Listen, would love to chat but I have to fly. Like, literally. My flight leaves in twenty minutes."

"You're leaving London today?" I ask in dismay.

"LA is calling, baby. But we'll get together again soon, right? Call me any time. Catch you later, red devil!"

Mum and Dad are both waiting in reception as I trudge out to join them. They both look weary and anxious. I try to summon a smile, but it's difficult.

"We'll make this work, Storm," says Mum as we drive back to the hotel. "We have to make it work." I think she says this last part to herself.

In reception, Dad picks up an evening paper. He puts it down again quickly. Automatically I reach for it too.

I stare at the picture of a girl in a cheesy black hoodie and Union Jack flip-flops, her hair pulled tightly back with an elastic band and cheap sunnies perched on her nose. The washing label on her handbag is flapping in the wind.

STORM IN TURBULENCE?

Is the pressure of fame getting to Jase's new squeeze? "That girl should sack her stylist," says an unnamed source. "She looks like a hobo." Sources close to Storm suggest that her hard-partying lifestyle is getting too much for the fifteen-year-old wannabe pop star. Will her career be no more than a storm in a teacup?

Dad gently prises the paper from my clenched fingers.

"We'll figure this out, love," he says. "I promise."

CHAPTER 20

I stand and smile and hold my drink tightly in one hand. I think it's cherry, but all I've got to go on is that it's red.

Eric and Derek are giggling and snorting over their sparkling water. I keep smiling because I don't know what else to do, apart from watch the doors in the hope that Jase might appear. I checked his itinerary before we came out and it said Tokyo, so the chances of him turning up here are slim to none. Still, I keep hoping. There's nothing else to do.

"Baby girl," says Eric. He slips his heavily beringed hand through the crook of my elbow and winks at me. "This must be *awfully* exciting for you. And did I tell you already how sensational you look?"

"I told you that dress would suit her," says Derek.

I try not to adjust the dress where it's cutting into my waist and take another sip of my drink. Urgh. Definitely not cherry. My feet are hurting in these shoes. They are higher than anything I've worn before. Eric and Derek have been telling me all night that they make me look taller and slimmer.

"Hey, Storm! It's so good to see you!"

"Er," I say, staring at a guy I've never seen before.

"I'm *loving* the outfit," says the Mystery Man. He strokes the gold fringing on the edge of my top. "So *edgy*. You're a fan of Maleesh Clubwear?"

"Maleesh Clubwear?" I ask, my mind racing. "I don't really know—"

Luckily, Eric butts in, saving me. "She absolutely adores it!" he cries. I realize a little late that Mystery Man's holding a little black Dictaphone in one hand. Eric scoffs, "Why else would she be at the Maleesh Clubwear launch?"

Oops. I probably should have known that. I take another sip of my drink. It isn't improving. Without Jase to have fun with, this party is actually quite boring.

"Simply *everyone* has been asking about her clothes," Eric continues, prattling on. "Why, she's wearing Maleesh Clubwear head to foot tonight!"

Derek and Eric didn't tell me that when they dressed me. I smile and try not to look as if it's news.

"Echo Music supports Maleesh Clubwear in all its endeavours," adds Derek.

"Especially given that Maleesh is sponsoring Jinxxy's new tour?" the man asks.

The words to that stupid Jinxxy song come straight back into my head.

"*All* its endeavours," Derek repeats firmly.

I look at my phone. It's almost eleven o'clock and time for my lift home. I can hardly wait to leave tonight. I think of Mum and Dad waiting patiently for me outside in the car, and feel a little rush of love and gratitude for them both.

Ping.

Tokyo is loco-kyo! No one here to talk to tho.

Missing you!

Jase xx

How incredible to be in Japan, I think, picturing Jase in the neon wonderland of Tokyo. Now I've signed with Echo, I'm going to have an amazing career just like his. It's going to be exciting and money-spinning and travelicious and . . . and. . .

Lonely.

Ping.

Call me, baby girl, things to discuss!

Adrian

I move as fast as my shoes will allow to a quieter corner of the room.

"Adrian?"

"Good party?" says my producer.

"Great," I lie.

"I have some thrilling news for you, Storm. Are you sitting down?"

198

I sit down obediently. It's not easy in my Maleesh Clubwear dress.

"We are flying in an entire team from LA to get behind your career," says Adrian in triumph. "They have worked with everyone you can imagine – Katy Perry, Taylor Swift, Meghan Trainor – and they cannot *wait* to meet you. Isn't that wonderful?"

I feel a bit dazed. The names may be a little too poppy for my tastes, but there's no denying that they are heavyweights. "That's amazing, Adrian," I say. "Thank you."

"So all we have to do is fix up a meeting when they fly in the day after tomorrow and you, my darling, will be making number ones around the GLOBE. Can you do Thursday?"

If the meeting's going to be on Thursday, this must be Tuesday. It's weird how the days are blurring together. Something is happening on Saturday next week – I can't remember exactly what – but I think this Thursday is clear.

"Have you checked with my mum?" I ask.

"I'm going to assume you can do Thursday," Adrian says. "It's going to be *so* exciting. We'll say ten o'clock."

"Yes, but Mum—"

Adrian interrupts with an impatient sigh. "Darling, the last thing the team from LA is going to want is your mother hanging around. 'Momagers' are more trouble than they're worth. If we're going to make your career happen, then you're going to have to rethink your management."

"Rethink it?" I repeat blankly. "How?"

"Get rid of your mother."

I can't actually speak. This can't be happening. I've lost Dad already. I can't get rid of Mum too. She's my last link to reality.

"Are you serious?" I croak at last.

"Having your mother in the driving seat makes you seem amateur. This team are professionals. You have to trust me when I tell you that this the only way to send your career into the stratosphere, where it belongs."

I think about Ivy Baxter's advice in Hawaii, back

when all this began: *You have to do what's right for you, no matter what. No apologies.*

I swallow. "OK," I say in a voice that doesn't feel like it belongs to me.

"Good. We'll say ten o'clock on Thursday, OK? Have fun with Eric and Derek now. Oh, and make sure you talk to everyone about Maleesh Clubwear. They are a very important sponsor for Echo right now."

I stay where I am for a few minutes after he rings off, gazing at my phone with blurry eyes. I have to get rid of Mum as my manager or my career won't move forward. This is the worst thing that's ever happened. The worst decision I've ever had to make.

I dial Belle's number.

"Pick up," I whisper. "Please, Belle, please, please. . ."

No answer. I slide my phone back into my bag and stand up from my stool and head towards the doors, where the most difficult conversation of my life is waiting patiently for me in a car. I get about halfway across the dance floor when I break down in tears that just won't stop. A couple of people take pictures. It's not hard to guess what the headlines will be in the tabloids tomorrow.

When did all this get so *hard*?

CHAPTER 21

On Thursday morning, I am sitting on my own in the hotel. Everything is quiet, as my family have all gone home. I've got so used to the noise of my little brothers flying from one side of the suite to the other armed with dinosaurs that the silence feels unnatural.

I don't want to think about the conversation I had with Mum on Tuesday night. I don't want to think about that ever again.

I have half an hour to decide on my outfit and another half an hour before the taxi takes me to Echo Music to meet my new team. There's so much Maleesh Clubwear stuff in this cupboard now that it's pushing everything else on to the floor and making me feel a bit cross-eyed. I reach in and grab an armful of stuff. Shut the door with my foot, dump the stuff on the bed and study it for a few minutes. If I can't pull an outfit together out of this lot, then I'm not the style queen I thought I was.

Storm Hall @stormhall_official
How to choose? @maleesh #fashion #music

To help me concentrate, I pull my hair back and secure it with a scrunchy. It's still long and blond, but if Eric and Derek have their way it won't stay like that. Every time I go in to the office, they eye it and exchange significant glances. I hope the LA team think I should keep it long.

You don't mean that.

Don't think about Mum.

I grab a tee, and a belt, and a pair of pleather leggings. A jacket, a necklace.

I hope this works out for you, Storm.

I throw the jacket on the floor and pick up another. Still Mum is marching through my head.

They'll take advantage of you. They'll turn you into someone that you're not.

Jacket: yes. Leggings: yes. Shoes or boots or trainers or heels?

It's your choice. I hope it makes you happy.

I set the clothing combination neatly on a chair, pull on my trainers and my favourite running outfit. I select a pair of sunglasses that are cool but not too look-at-me. Grabbing my keys and my phone, I slide my sunglasses on to my nose and take the lift.

People look up from their papers as I pass them in reception. I head out of the doors, breaking into a jog right away and taking the paps by surprise. By the time they've twigged, I'm round the corner and heading through the park. Luckily, they probably assume I've arranged a ride somewhere, because they don't bother to follow.

I aim for a bench under some trees near the Albert Memorial, where I sit and watch the squirrels for a while. There are loads here, silvery and bright-eyed, flowing up and down the tree trunks like furry water.

Taking out my phone, I check it without much hope. Plenty of tweets asking me for follows, to promote stuff, to come to parties all over town. Nothing from Belle. Nothing from Jase. The last time I heard from him was the text from Tokyo two days ago, at that Maleesh party. Missing me? I don't think so.

Did I really only meet Jase two weeks ago? The conversations, the texts, they all feel as if they happened to someone else.

I rest my head in my hands for a few minutes. Then I stand up and run back to the hotel for a shower and a quick change. I shouldn't keep my LA team waiting.

Cyndi from the LA is tiny and skinny and wearing an unlikely pair of velvet dungarees that would look awful on anyone else. The other members of her team – Sheree, Ali and Mo – are playing around with laptops and making calls and prowling from one end of the conference room to the other. Adrian and the Echo lawyers lounge around on the spinny conference chairs, swinging lightly from side to side. I feel like a wounded warthog in the middle of a pack of bored lions.

"The hair has to go," Cyndi says.

"Told you," Eric says to Derek, who smiles darkly.

"The hair is staying," says Adrian.

It's all going to be fine, I'm telling myself. I've said this to myself so many times today it's turned into an earwormy mantra that I can't turn off.

"We have to ask ourselves," Adrian continues. "What do kids today want?"

"Good music?" I offer.

"An original look, a thigh gap, a wardrobe and a lifestyle," Cyndi says over me.

Sheree and Ali look impressed. Mo writes it down.

Adrian gets out of his chair, comes up behind me and places his hands on my shoulders. I'm so tense, they must feel like rocks under his hands.

"Let's leave the look and talk about the music for a while," he says. "Now, we have booked studio time for you starting right after our meeting, baby girl. We don't have much time to put this together. Are you ready to put in the hours?"

"You can completely rely on me for that," I say, with the first stab of confidence I've felt since stepping back into the Echo offices. I can't wait to get into a recording booth and really show these guys what I can do.

"A great sound will complement your great look and make something unforgettable," Adrian continues.

"I totally agree. The sound is going to be perfect, I promise."

"Funny name, Stork," I hear Cyndi say to Mo. "I wouldn't have said she's tall enough to carry that off."

I feel my confidence waver. They think I'm called *Stork*?

"'Shrimp' would work better," Mo hisses in reply, giggling.

"Happy, baby girl?" says Adrian, chucking me under the chin.

It occurs to me that Adrian has never called me by my name. Not once. Baby girl, honey, darling, but never Storm.

"Adrian," I say awkwardly. "I think there's been a mix-up. You see, my name is Storm, not Stork."

"Great!" Adrian pats me on the cheek and heads back to talk to the lawyers.

What if I just walked out of here? I wonder suddenly. Would anyone notice?

The answer is, apparently, no.

Outside the conference room, I have no idea where to go next. It's suddenly horribly clear that I am nothing to these people. A starlet with no name, here today and gone tomorrow. A Stork.

The big white sofa in Adrian's office has just enough space below it for me to crawl underneath. I lie there miserably, hoping no one is going to come looking for me, while also hoping that everyone is wondering where I've gone. I need darkness and silence for a few minutes, so I can get my head straight.

I claw my phone out of my back pocket and lift it up to my nose. Find my Facebook page. I need to feel connected to the real world.

Parties, picnics, selfies in the mall, face-pulling in the school corridors. I drink in the pictures like a thirsty person at a water cooler. I pore over snaps of Jade and Belle, Colin and Sanjit, Daniel and Bonnie and even the Grim Twins themselves, Gwen and Emily Douglas. Life is going on without me. No one misses me. I have no friends, no family. Just my career. It doesn't feel enough somehow.

I ring Jase one last hopeless time.

"Hey," I mumble when he picks up. "Are you in the UK?"

I hear him call at someone in the background: "Is Birmingham in the UK?" Then he comes back to me. "Yes, a couple hours from London. How's it going with Echo?"

I don't want to whine and sound unprofessional so I just say "Everything's great!" in a cheery voice which sounds like I caught my finger in a zipper.

"Awesome! Listen, wanna hang out and do something cool tonight?"

If Jase still wants to hang out with me, perhaps I'm so not alone after all.

"I'd love that," I say gratefully.

"Awesome. Call you later!"

CHAPTER 22

"*Dance with me,*" I sing into the mic. "*Dance so close and—*"

"Not working for me," interrupts Adrian in my headphones. "You have to sound sexier, baby girl."

I bite back a remark about being only fifteen. This is a professional environment and I can't let my age count against me. I try and adjust my voice, make it huskier.

"Flowers twi-i-ining through the beat. . ."

"You sound like Marilyn Monroe after too many cigarettes, darling." Adrian is starting to sound testy, and it's making my palms sweat. "Take it again."

I grip the mic with my hands as best I can.

Looking bored, the session musicians restart the intro. We're going faster than I want, but Adrian thinks the tempo I worked out with the guys in Glasgow is too dirgey and funereal.

We almost make it to the end when Adrian cuts in again.

"We're having second thoughts in here, Storm," he says.

I wipe my forehead and take a sip of water. How long have I been in here? It feels like hours and we're only on the second track.

"What second thoughts?" I ask cautiously.

Cyndi looms over Adrian's shoulder in the mixing room. "Second thoughts about the song," she says. "Don't you have something more upbeat?"

"This is upbeat," I try to explain. "It's supposed to be funky and—"

"It's as funky as a dead dog," Cyndi says bluntly. "Where's the hook? Where's the part that says to me, I wanna dance to this track?"

"It's a different kind of funky, Cyndi," I say hopelessly. "The kind that gets into your heartbeat."

"Honey, it's not doing it. What else have we got?"

I'm doing my best to stay positive here, but it's hard. "Dance with Me" is one of the best songs I've ever written.

"Actually, we have a song here you could sing," says Cyndi. "It's a little Europop, a touch of electro-house, a great combination, it's really going to suit our market. We're going to play it for you, have a listen. I think you'll be excited."

The electro Europop is called "Pop Until U Stop" and is every bit as bad as it sounds. I watch Adrian and Cyndi bobbing their heads up and down like pigeons. It would be funny if it wasn't so awful.

"I don't think this genre really suits my voice," I say when the track ends and they look at me with expectant faces. "I have another track we could try, it's pretty cool—"

"Sing the song and we'll make the decision, baby girl," says Adrian. The tone of his voice reminds me of Mum when she's not going to take no for an answer.

Don't think about Mum.

I sing the song, if you can call it singing. Cyndi's team gather around Adrian as they loop and link and layer the sounds the way they want them. I stand in the corner, waiting for someone to ask my opinion. No one does.

"When can we break for lunch?" I ask.

Cyndi looks at my stomach. It's sticking out a bit thanks to the extra bread roll I had with my breakfast in a bid to cheer myself up today.

"We need to talk nutrition, Storm," she says. "Teenage girls are very body conscious. It's so important to give them the right message."

I suck my stomach in. "And the right message is the importance of eating a proper lunch?" I say.

Cyndi dismisses the question with a wave of her hand. "Later," she says. "We still have too much work to do. Adrian, the second section needs more *grind*, don't you agree?"

I'm starting to hate this recording booth. The headphones are hurting my ears and it's hot and airless. We do five more takes of "Pop Until U Stop". If this goes on much longer, I'm the one who'll be popping.

"We're starting to pull this together," says Cyndi three hours later. "Take a break, everyone!"

I take my headphones off with a sigh. I was only watching squirrels in the park this morning, but it feels like *years* ago. I've forgotten what daylight looks like.

"Can we have a word?" says Cyndi. She pushes me down into a chair. Mo, Sheree and Ali gather round. "Has anyone raised the question of your nose?" Cyndi says.

I like my nose. I can breathe through it and everything.

"What's wrong with it?" I ask defensively.

Cyndi shakes her head. "It's crooked. Off centre. This kind of disfigurement plays havoc in publicity shots."

Disfigurement seems like a strong word. I reach my hand nervously towards my face.

"Some minor rhinoplasty and you'll see that it's the tiny adjustments that make all the difference," Cyndi goes on.

"Rhinoplasty?" I echo. "You mean, a nose job?"

"It's very minor, and pretty much everyone gets it done at some point. You'll think about it? We'll be needing those publicity shots soon. Now, do you need anything?"

"A sandwich would be nice," I say longingly.

Cyndi clicks her tongue. "We'll do a few more takes and talk about food later. Adrian, are we good to go again?"

By the time I am allowed to leave the Echo recording studio, my head feels as light as a cloud. I knew life as a recording artist would be tough, but today was a lot tougher than I was expecting.

A taxi scoops me up before any of the paps that hang around the doors of Echo realize it's me and I'm whisked back through a darkened London to my hotel. My big, quiet hotel. No Mum, no Dad, no Tina, no kid brothers. Just me and a LOT of Maleesh Clubwear.

I call room service and order their biggest sandwich. It tastes incredible. When I've eaten so much I can't squeeze in another bite, I lie down on my bed and stare at the ceiling.

"This is working life," I tell myself. "Get used to it."

Mum will want to know how I got on today, I tell myself. She may not be my manager any more, but she's still my mother. I find that I can't wait to call her.

"I'm going out, Storm," Mum says when I get through. "Is this important?"

I can hear Jake and Alex screaming in the background, Dad's gruff voice and even the distant notes of music coming from Tina's room. My stomach twists with longing. I want to say: Of course it's important! It's my LIFE! But I don't because I know Mum is still mad at me and I have to prove that I'm doing OK without her. What's the point in poking an angry bear? Way more sensible to keep your distance.

"Just checking in," I say as casually as I can. "I've been recording today and it's sounding awesome. Everything OK up there?"

"Fine. You?"

There is so much to say and I can't say any of it.

"Yes," I say quietly. "Everything's great."

I try Belle next.

"What do you want, Storm?"

Her voice is flat. Flat, with Belle, means dangerous.

"Do I have to want anything to call you? I miss my bestie! We've barely had a chance to talk lately," I say, as brightly as I can.

"Which part of our last conversation don't you remember?" she responds. "The part about you not needing my advice, or the part about me not digging you out of any more holes?"

"Look, I really appreciate that you have my interests at heart. Really, I do. So I'm sorry if I—"

"Storm," Belle repeats, "what do you want?"

I need to hear a friendly voice.

"Oh, you know," I say, flustered. "To have a bit of a catch-up. Maybe a giggle." I want more than just a phone call, I want to be in the same room with her. It seems like everyone I care about has been reduced to a voice in a phone.

"I needed to talk to you about the party and you never called me back."

"I know, and I'm sorry," I say. "Really. It won't

happen again. And there isn't that much to tell; those pictures of me and Jase and Harry were pretty much the extent of it."

There's a pause before Belle says, "Not that party, Storm."

"Oh," I say, starting to feel irritated. "Well, I go to a LOT of parties these days. How am I supposed to know which one you mean?"

Silence.

"Belle?"

There's only so many times a girl can take a friend hanging up on her. I think I just reached my limit. Wiping away angry tears, I dial Jase. No answer. I check my watch. Eight o'clock. I need to be recording again at Echo by seven tomorrow morning. If Jase and I are going to hang out, we need to start pretty soon.

I call down to reception.

"Has anyone left a message for me?"

The receptionist reels off the names of a few tabloid-type journos and three fashion labels wanting to get me along to promo parties.

"I mean, any personal messages?"

"Nothing, Miss Hall."

Trying to get ready for a date with a megastar at the same time as trying to *contact* said megastar is exhausting. After the day I've had, I feel like crying by the time I reach my fifth outfit (Maleesh again) and my fifth engaged tone on the phone. It's almost nine o'clock.

Storm Hall @stormhall_official

Can't wait to see you 2nite? @jasem4real

Jase, where are U? Meet me at the hotel? Storm

xxx

I snap pictures of myself in my Maleesh stuff and upload them alongside phrases like "All dressed up and nowhere to go!" and "Bring on the dancing! #maleesh". Where is he? Was I imagining our date tonight?

Finally, I get through to Angie on Jase's PR team. I like Angie, she's always been nice to me on the few occasions that I've met her.

"Hi, Angie," I say in relief, sinking on to the bed. "Do you know where Jase is? We were supposed to be meeting tonight."

"Jase had to fly to Reykjavik at short notice," says Angie. "Didn't he tell you?"

"Oh," I say. There isn't anything else TO say, really. "No, he didn't."

"I'm sorry," Angie says. "Perhaps he'll call you later?"

And perhaps the moon will fall out of the sky, I think as I hang up. I put down my phone beside my bed and sit there for a while, gazing at my reflection in the wardrobe mirror opposite the end of my bed. Look at me. Dressed to kill and no one to murder.

There's no one else I can think of to talk to, apart from Colin Park. And that would be weird, because we haven't really spoken in months AND he's Belle's boyfriend. It shows how desperate I'm getting.

The soft tones of the Brink waft into my ears from the radio I have playing in the hotel bathroom.

Call me any time.

CHAPTER 23

"I'm sorry it's so late," I say nervously as I perch on the chair in Leo Greenwood's office.

"I work strange hours," Leo tells me. "Same as my clients. What can I do for you, Storm? You sounded worried on the phone."

I wrap my hands around the comfy leather armrests on the chair and try to relax. Good music is playing. The kind of music I want to sing. The sort of world I want to be a part of, a world that's a universe away from where I have somehow found myself.

"I really need to get out of this," I blurt. I hand him a smudgy copy of my Echo contract. "Can you help me?"

Leo flips through the contract. Laying it on the desk, he steeples his fingers together. "Echo are a reputable label," he says. "They have plenty of success stories and a bank balance that many other labels would kill for. Are you sure you want to throw that away?"

I think of Jinxxy.

"They're trying to make me something I'm not," I say. "Mr Greenwood—"

"Leo," he says. "Please."

"Leo, I'm not a pop star. I thought I could be, but I was wrong. I want to be a real musician singing real music, not a sampled, autotuned clothes hanger. I can't sing the music Echo want me to sing. I thought that perhaps I could make it work, but I know now that they are completely wrong for me. I feel like such an idiot."

Warm tears have started flowing down my cheeks. Leo pushes a box of tissues towards me and I blow my nose.

"I can't believe I threw away Sound Pacific," I groan. "I honestly don't know what happened.

One minute I was so excited because Enrique Diablo liked me and the next minute I was signing something completely different with people I hardly knew. I think Echo never even heard my music, even though Jase said he'd played it to them and they thought it was good. Everything ran away from me." I pull out a few more tissues. "You must think I'm really stupid."

"Not stupid. Just young." He raises his hand as I open my mouth to protest. "There's no shame in being young, Storm. But it's important to recognize your limits sometimes and know when to stop and ask for help."

"So can you help me?" I ask.

"What do your parents think?"

"I tried to call Mum earlier. She was busy and didn't want to talk to me. I'm not surprised, to be honest."

Leo waits tactfully as I cry for a few seconds and use up half the box of tissues in one go. Then he makes soothing noises that make me cry harder for a while. I'm so *tired*.

"We'll tackle this a step at a time," he says as I shudder and gulp at the air.

He starts talking through the contract. There are lots of details I don't remember, about sponsors and rights and copyright. I never even read the thing before I signed it, I remember with a flush of shame. I didn't want to embarrass Jase, or to look like I had never done anything like sign a contract before.

"You do know, Storm," says Leo, voicing my biggest fear, "that if you break this contract with Echo, you may end up with no record company at all? It's very unlikely that Sound Pacific will take you back."

No record company. No career. My throat feels dry and painful at the thought. I think about what breaking with Echo might really mean. I've been incredibly lucky to get this deal. Am I mad to be ditching them? Then I think about "Pop Until U Stop". About Maleesh, and short hair, and rhinoplasty. Stork.

"I'd prefer to risk it," I say at last. "I never want

to feel as bad again as I have over these last couple of days."

"Good," says Leo. "Then I'll do what I can. If there's a loophole, I'm going to find it. Now, go back to your hotel and get some rest. We'll talk again tomorrow."

I let Leo call me a cab. I let him open the door, and I let him pay the cabbie and tell the cabbie where to go. It's so wonderful to know that, finally, someone sensible is in charge.

A couple of paps are waiting by the hotel, looking bored. I clamp my sunglasses on my nose even though it's dark outside because I don't want my red eyes splashed all over the papers tomorrow. Then I jump into a lift and lean my head against the door as it closes. It's been a loooong day.

My phone rings.

"S'up? Are you around?"

I feel a bit stunned at the sound of Jase's growly voice. Angie was right. He called me. A bit later than I was expecting, but a call is a call, right?

"I thought you were in Reykjavik?" I say.

"Baby, I was. Cold as hell. I told them I couldn't stick those temperatures and took the first flight back to the UK. I'm in London right now. Do you want to party?"

Just because I'm thinking of breaking with Echo doesn't mean I have to break off all contact with Jase, does it? And after my conversation with Leo, maybe I have something to party about after all.

"Isn't it kind of late?" I ask.

"Superstars like us party till dawn! I'll pick you up in forty minutes."

Thirty-nine minutes later, I'm pacing around the reception area, feeling tense. Forty-nine minutes later, the same thing. Also fifty-nine minutes. At ten past midnight, I am almost asleep in one of the reception area's comfy chairs when I feel a hand on my shoulder.

"Baby girl," says Jase. "Ready to have fun?"

I let him pull me to my feet. He gives me a big smooch on one cheek, then angles his phone to get a picture of us together.

"Quick before the crazies figure out I'm here," he says.

I rub my eyes. "Who are the crazies?"

"Weird girls who stalk me around town. Come on."

He's already too late. Three girls in Jase T-shirts are running down the street towards the hotel as we walk towards the waiting Bentley. My stomach tightens as I recognize Biro Girl.

Two burly bodyguards appear from nowhere to hold back what has already become a crowd. Something hits me. An egg, its broken shell and oozy innards dribbling down my T-shirt as I half fall into the car. If I was half asleep before, I'm wide awake now.

Biro Girl has her fingers hooked over the partially open window now, and she's yelling something about leaving Jase alone. The window closes after what feels like for ever. There are flashes through the windows, and faces crushed up against the glass.

"Get us out of here, man," Jase tells the driver.

I shake as we drive, trying my best to wipe the egg off my top. I'm guessing it's a present from Biro Girl. Belle would probably find it hilarious.

My stomach clenches at the thought of Belle.

"Don't worry about the mess." Jase looks totally unbothered by the chaos we just left behind. "My people will have a whole new outfit for you to wear when we arrive."

"How do you put up with it?" I ask.

"Goes with the territory, I guess."

We ride in silence for a while, while Jase scrolls through his phone.

"Do you have any friends, Jase?" I ask.

He looks startled. "Sure I have friends. I have friends all over the world."

I think about Belle. "I mean *real* friends," I say quietly. "Friends who've known you since you were a kid. Friends who tell you when you're being an idiot."

Jase considers the question. "I've got a friend from middle school," he says. "But we've kinda lost touch lately. You know how it is."

"That's sad," I say.

Jase grins at me. "Do I look sad?"

He does, I suddenly realize. Underneath all the swagger, he's the saddest guy I've ever met.

More paps and more screaming fans are waiting when we arrive at the store where the party is being held. I think I glimpse Biro Girl at the back of the crowd. She must have a scooter or something, to cover the distances. I hide the egg mess as best I can in the burst of flash photography that follows our arrival. I'm so glad to see the new clothes that I practically snatch them out of Jase's PR woman Angie's hands. There are perks to this life, I guess, even if they come in the eternal form of Maleesh clubwear.

By the time I have changed and sorted out my make-up again, Jase has vanished. I fetch myself a drink and try to smile and look casual in the press of people milling around the store.

The trouble is, when you try to look casual, you end up looking anything BUT casual. I try to adjust the way I'm standing, and wobble in my shoes. I'm too tired to react in time to stop myself falling. So I end up grabbing a store mannequin around the neck and we crash to the ground in a shower of plastic limbs.

This is possibly the worst night of my life.

Angie helps me to my feet. I try to keep my head turned away as people laugh and take pictures. Music booms on and I still can't see Jase.

"I . . . I banged my head," I say, frantically choking back tears. "Please, Angie . . . I want to go home." Home to Glasgow, home to Mum and Dad, home to my cosy bed and my teddies (laugh if you dare) and my family and my friends.

Angie sorts out a taxi to take me back to the hotel. I don't see Jase to say goodbye.

CHAPTER 24

News 4 Youz @news4youz
Is the pressure getting to @stormhall_official?
@jasem4real needs to teach this girl a thing or
two about the world of fame! #fail

Celebrity News @celebnewsstories
BREAKING NEWS @stormhall_official and
@jasem4real on the rocks, and not in a cocktail
kinda way! More when we have it

Elena Novak @qweenmahunny
STILL WAITING JASE!!!! ♥♥♥

It's amazing what a bang to the head can do. As
the cab drives along London's deserted streets, I find
a whole lot of things coming properly into focus
for the first time in ages. Not counting Jase – who
I'm going to delete from my phone as soon as I get
round to it – I have precisely three problems that
need sorting out: Echo, friends and family. Leo is
sorting out Echo. It's up to me to sort out the rest.

One thing is chasing round and round in my
head as I get wearily into bed. *Just because something
is hard, doesn't mean you can't manage it.*

I have to do everything in my power to win my
friends and family back. I know it's not going to be
easy. I dropped them all for the sake of my so-called

career. They aren't going to let me pick them up again like nothing's happened. How can I repair the damage I've done? How?

There isn't much point in trying to sleep any more, I realize, as the birds start twittering in the trees outside my hotel window. Today is potentially the most important day of my life. It might as well start now.

The very first thing I do when I open my tired eyes is ignore my phone. There is no time for a "morning, world!" selfie. Not today. Instead, I yank open the wardrobe. When did I end up with so many clothes? Even *I* don't need this many clothes. I start tugging stuff from shelves and hooks, racks and rails, and piling it up by my feet. Don't need it, don't like it, nope, nope, nope, nope – OK, maybe – nope, nope, nope.

The more stuff that ends up on the floor, the more energized I feel. This is like a clothes workout. I should make a DVD. Scoop and chuck! Scoop, grab, unfold and CHUCK!

Half an hour later, I sit down, panting slightly,

and look at the mess on the floor. I have reduced the contents of the hotel cupboard by about seventy-five per cent. It's an amazing feeling, to be able once again to see the things that I truly, genuinely *like* among all the freebies that have been cluttering the view.

I call reception, order a room service breakfast and ask for as many plastic bags as they can find. I'm filled with purpose and toast and tea and it feels good.

Next, I put the piles of clothes into all the bags and stack them up. Within five minutes of calling down to reception again, three guys in hotel uniform have appeared at my door and cleared the lot, with strict instructions to give everything to a local charity shop as soon as the shops open. From the looks they give me as they stagger out with the bags, it's clear that they think I'm mad. I don't care. I feel powerful and in charge of my own life again. This must be what a snake feels like when it sloughs off its tight old skin, or Rita Ora when she unveils a radical new look.

I eat more toast and call Leo.

"I think we have something," he tells me. "I'm working on it right now."

"Thank you," I say gratefully. "Echo are expecting me to be at the studio this morning by nine. If you can work out something by then, it would be amazing and I would love you for ever."

"We're more likely to have something this afternoon, but I'll keep you posted. You're sounding much better today, by the way."

"I feel like a different person."

"Not too different, I hope?"

"Different enough," I say.

I have a long shower, and then enjoy selecting an outfit to get me through the rest of my day. No Maleesh, just all my favourite labels. As I pull the jacket I bought with Belle from Topshop the day we went to Jase's concert off its hanger, I remember with a pang how we felt as we danced together around the personal shopping area in the store. When Jase was a hero, not a real guy I've got to know. When Belle and I were friends, and when

Echo was nothing at all. I want that feeling back. I can't believe I nearly let it go.

A glimmer of a song washes through me. I stop twirling, and try to hold the thought. Time, the past, wanting things back to how they were. I'm going too fast, I realize.

Dropping the jacket hastily on the bed before the idea can slide out of my brain, I sit down at the hotel desk and open the drawer. I've never used hotel paper before. A song for Belle is as good a place to start as any. A song to show her how sorry I am, how much I miss her. A song in her words. What she would say to me now . . . if I hadn't pushed her away.

> *Give yourself a little time, time*
> *Give yourself a little time*
> *Time is passing you by, this you can't deny*
> *Stop wishing to be someone you're not and*
>   *celebrate all that you got*
> *We're so pressured to be bigger better braver*
> *When you are your own saviour*
> *Give yourself a little time*

I pick out a melody, fitting it to the words. It feels good and strong, and about as far from "Pop Until U Stop" as it could be, so I take out my phone and start recording phrases, softly at first and then with more confidence as I feel the song taking shape. I can't believe how quickly it's coming. I already know the title: "Time".

Love
You gotta stop and feel the love
Gotta hold on to what you got
Never give it up

The sound of my phone jolts me out of my fragile sound world. I lay down my pen reluctantly and pick up.

"It's ten past nine," says Adrian. He sounds mad. "Everyone is here and waiting. Where are you?"

Ten past *nine*? Eek! Adrian goes on about professionalism for a while, but all I can hear are the words to Belle's song.

"If you can't handle the pressure this early in

your career, it's going to spell disaster for you when the work really starts—"

Share
When you're down, just look and share
Lots of people wanna take care
You're one of a kind

"—Cyndi has a dozen other debut artists on her books who want her time and input. . ."

Believe, all you gotta do is believe

"—and the publicity slots need to be planned well in advance, but if we have no album, then we'll have to go back to the drawing board—"

I have to go in. I'm still under contract, and I know from what Leo told me about the details that things could turn nasty for me if I don't.

"I'm coming," I interrupt. "Please apologize to the team for me. I've been writing a new song, I'll play it to you if—"

"Get here as quickly as you can."

Take control and you will see
Destiny is here

I make it to the office in twenty-five minutes. Cyndi, Mo, Ali, Sheree, Erik and Derek all look at me with expressions ranging from lack of interest to mild irritation.

"I'm really sorry I'm late," I say, breathless from running up the stairs because the lift took too long. "I got caught up in a song I'm writing which I think might be really good. Can I sing it for you?"

"We don't have time," says Adrian.

"We need you in the booth right now," Cyndi says, checking her watch.

My all-powerful mood from earlier is disappearing faster than bathwater down a plughole. "Please, I just want to sing it to you really quickly, that would be OK, right?"

"It might have been OK if you'd got here at nine," says Adrian testily. "But it's ten o'clock now. Mo? Where's the new song?"

It's another poppy track along similar lines to

"Pop Until U Stop". In fact, it pretty much IS "Pop Until U Stop". I'm singing the aural equivalent of Spot the Difference in Jake and Alex's comics.

I walk into the booth and settle the headphones on my head. They feel heavier than yesterday, somehow.

Leo, I beg inside my head as I start singing all the oohs and yeahs and whoos that they want. *Get me out of here, Leo. I'm depending on you!*

CHAPTER 25

"Storm? Can you take 'Boom La La' again from the top? We need it to be sexier."

"Boom la la," I sing dully as another piece of me dies inside. Is this the fourth or the fifth track we've worked on today? They all have stupid names ("It's important to keep the words neutral for our international market") and I hate each one more than the last.

"That's about as sexy as a bundle of sticks, Storm. We need you to feel this music, OK? There's a gorgeous guy and you're singing these words because there's no other way of articulating how great he makes you feel. Got that?"

This guy must be a real doozy.

"Boom la la," I try again. I wiggle my butt in the hope that it'll make me feel sexier but I just feel stupid. "Ooh, boom, boom baby, yeah boom boom honey, boom la la boom."

I'm desperate to stop singing this plastic song and feel like me again. The me I want to be, that is. The me who writes proper heartfelt songs and sings them with pride. I check my phone every time Adrian calls a break. I check it when I run to the bathroom, I check it when I'm at the water cooler, I check it and check it. It's two o'clock now. I've been working flat out for four hours. *Call me, Leo.*

At half past four, a runner from the office joins Adrian, Cyndi and the others on the other side of the glass. Everyone looks round, and I am forgotten. I sink down on to my haunches and rest my head in my hands.

Adrian swings back to look at me. He leans into the mic.

"Can you come out here for a minute, baby?"

I wearily flop on to the sofa beside the mixing desk. An autotuned, pumping version of my voice loops around me.

"Your lawyer," Adrian says. He doesn't look pleased. "He's coming in. Says he wants to meet us right now. Do you have any idea what it could be about?"

I beam with relief. Leo has something. Finally!

"No idea," I say happily.

Cyndi has a face like a prune. "Lawyers spell one thing, honey. Trouble. Our schedule cannot accommodate too many more interruptions like this."

"I guess that's how it goes," I say. "And it's STORM, not 'honey', by the way," I add cheerfully. "Please try and remember."

News 4 Youz @news4youz
What's this we hear about @stormhall_official breaking with @EchoMusicLtd? Whatever you say about Jase's girl, she's never dull!

NME @nme

Industry gripped by @EchoMusicLtd and the

latest news. #stormywaters

Celebrity News @celebnewsstories

Speculation re @EchoMusicLtd losing scalp

@stormhall_official. No comment from Echo's

big star @jasem4real #musicnews

Elena Novak @qweenmahunny

Im on my 1000th heart for you Jase

@jasem4real #biroheart #jasenelena4ever

I know it's Jase the moment he calls. I've still got his name programmed into my phone. You don't think I meant it when I said I was going to delete it? This is JASE MAHONE we're talking about here. And still completely gorgeous and into me in his own weird, megastarry way.

"Hey!" I say, my phone pressed between my ear and my shoulder as I sprawl on my hotel bed remote-surfing through the TV with one hand and munching on an apple with the other. I'm on three of the music channels.

"Is it true?" Jase demands. "You're breaking with Echo?"

"My lawyer found that I was working on an adult contract instead of a child one." I've never been so pleased to be under sixteen in my life.

"Are you insane?"

I blink. He sounds really mad.

"Jase, Echo and I weren't really getting on, so I—"

"Jeez, Storm, if I'd ditched Echo every time Adrian wound me up, I would not be the multimillion-selling recording artist I am today! Are you dumb or just naïve?"

Charming!

"This isn't your decision," I point out. "It's mine. I'm grateful that you fixed up the meeting with Adrian and—"

"I busted my neck to get you that deal!"

"I really am grateful," I repeat. "But when everything became clear, I had to do something."

"And when exactly did 'everything become clear'?"

I take a bite out of my apple. "Somewhere around the second verse of 'Pop Until U Stop'," I explain through my crunching. "I couldn't do it Echo's way. I have to find another deal, someone who'll suit my voice and – you know. *Get* me."

"Opportunities don't come along like buses, Storm."

I wonder when Jase Mahone last took a bus.

"If you'd stuck with me, I'd have guided you through it," he insists. "We could have recorded together, we could have toured, promoted. We could have made something really great. You should have trusted me. I've been in this business for three years, I know how it works."

"I can't stick with Echo," I repeat.

"I thought you liked me."

He sounds genuinely gutted. I wonder for the first time if perhaps I'm the first person he's ever counted as a friend since the middle-school buddy he told me about during the ride in the Bentley. It's weird to say it, but right now I'm actually feeling sorry for the guy.

"I do!" I say. "This is about Echo, not you. I don't want you to be mad at me, but I have to do this my way."

He sighs. "Fine," he says. "Do whatever you think is best, Storm. It's your life. But you can't say I didn't try."

I feel relieved. "Thanks. That means a lot. I'll call you later, OK?"

Leo calls me the moment Jase rings off.

"I can't believe we didn't spot the age thing sooner. Sometimes it's the big stuff that you miss, not the small print. Echo have agreed to release you. You're free, Storm. How do you feel?"

I contemplate the big, blank horizon unfolding in front of me. No more "Pop Until U Stop" is pretty fantastic, but. . .

"Scared," I admit. "What if I don't get another deal?"

"But if you're as good as Sound Pacific thought, something will come up."

"It would be nice if Sound Pacific gave me another chance," I say sadly. "But I guess there's no hope of that."

"Don't hold your breath," Leo agrees.

The reality of what I've done hits me as soon as Leo rings off. I'm adrift in a holey dinghy on a big, careerless sea. All the boasting I've done online, all the posing and the teasing about deals with Echo, deals with Sound Pacific, and now I have a big fat nothing. Zero. Zip. Nothing but life back in the classroom, the Douglas twins sneering at my failure and Belle not talking to me.

Feeling a rush of real fear, I call Jase back. He of all people will understand how I'm feeling.

"S'up? You are through to my voicemail. Leave a message so my people can call your people. Gotta fly!"

What's the point in rambling on record? I text him instead.

Chat some more? Storm xx

Come on, Jase. Be a friend, I think.

When ten minutes pass with no reply, I log on to Snapchat and message him that way. He doesn't open it. I can feel myself getting mad as I click through to Twitter. It won't let me send a message, even though I try three times. It finally dawns on me that he has unfollowed me. Snapchat, WhatsApp, Facebook, Twitter, Instagram. The whole lot.

I feel crushed.

Just when I needed him most, Jase Mahone has dumped me.

CHAPTER 26

If Jase Mahone doesn't want to talk to me, he doesn't have to. He has people who will talk to my people instead.

I thought he was better than that. I thought he liked me. But who am I kidding? Why would a superstar like Jase ever be interested in wee Storm Hall from Glasgow? Echo was just using him as bait. I wonder if he was trying to reel in Lauri B for Echo too. I have a vague memory of pics with her and Jase on Twitter a few weeks ago. But Lauri B was cleverer than me. She signed with Sound Pacific.

I can't believe it's taken me this long to realize that Jase Mahone was never my friend. Maybe Echo paid him to get me to sign with them. Promised him another tour, got him some great new sponsors. He didn't like me; he just liked what I might be able to get him. He said he liked my music, but he never mentioned the names of any of my songs. He said he'd played my stuff to Adrian, but Adrian never mentioned the name of any song either. No one listened because no one cared. No one was interested in the music. They were just interested in the image.

I switch off the TV and curl up into a tight, sad ball on my hotel bed. Belle warned me about Jase the first night we met, but I was too starry-eyed and full of my own self-importance to see it. All I could think was: of course Jase likes me! Of course he loves my music! Why wouldn't he? I'm so cool and pretty and talented! I'm @stormhall_official!

I sob into my pillow.

I am, officially, what Tina and Belle have been telling me for weeks.

An idiot.

My phone rings.

"Miss Hall? It's reception."

I rub my eyes and try to pull myself together. "Is there a package for me?" I ask, trying not to sound as if I have been crying.

"We were wondering when you would be checking out."

"Checking out?" I repeat.

The receptionist clears her throat. "Your, er, former representative at Echo Music called to cancel the room."

I feel a knot of anxiety in my stomach. Echo aren't responsible for me any more. I am entirely responsible for myself. I have five pounds twenty-three in my purse and about sixty pounds in a savings account. Something tells me that's not going to cover another night in this hotel.

I feel the first stirrings of genuine terror. It's getting dark and I have nowhere to stay tonight. I'm going to have to go out past the paps and bunk down on the bench in the park with the squirrels . . . or worse.

"How long do I have?" I ask.

The receptionist sounds uncomfortable. "Official checkout time was seven hours ago, Miss Hall."

I hang up and stare at my hotel bedroom. Even with all the stuff I got rid of this morning, there's a LOT to pack. I can't sleep on a park bench with this lot. I'll have to catch an overnight bus back to Glasgow, or maybe Leo would let me sleep on his couch.

My phone rings again. This time it's Mum.

"Your dad and I heard the news."

"Echo has cancelled the hotel room," I hiccup.

"What are you going to do?"

I sink to the carpet, completely and utterly overwhelmed by my situation.

"I don't know!" I sob. "I'm so sorry I've been an idiot, I'm so sorry that I wasted all your hard work and your money, I'm so sorry that I didn't realize what was happening until it was too late. I've well and truly screwed up. I've lost my only chance to make it, haven't I?"

"Probably."

Mum never was one to mince her words.

"Please, Mum," I groan. "Tell me what to do."

"Pack your things, get down to reception and check out of your room before they charge you for another night," Mum says.

I am hit by a fresh wave of frightened weeping. I don't want to sleep in the park. Bad things can happen to people who sleep in parks.

"Where you'll meet me, Dad, Tina, Jake and Alex," Mum continues. "We've booked ourselves a few cheaper rooms on the ground floor for tonight. We'll worry about tomorrow when it comes."

I stop crying. "You're . . . here?" I say weakly.

"Are you coming down or not?"

I pack my things in a kind of daze. My parents, my sister and my brothers aren't hundreds of miles away, up in Glasgow, turning their backs on the most useless member of the family. They are three floors down.

Three suitcases and one elevator ride later, and I'm falling into Dad's arms. Well, to be more accurate, I'm falling over my suitcase because it's right in between me and my family and I kind of forget about it being there until it's too late. I hadn't fastened properly it in my haste to get downstairs either, so now it's spilled an embarrassing quantity of dirty laundry on the chequered reception floor.

"Typical," says Tina as everyone rushes around to pull me back on to my feet. Mum rounds up the tangle of clothes, although Jake and Alex manage to grab a pair of knickers. They run around the reception area waving them and yelling for a bit.

"Right," says Mum, a bit out of breath after the boys have been trapped in a corner behind a large plant pot and the knickers have been forcibly removed from Alex's sweaty little hands and I have checked out of my room and Dad has apologized to everyone in reception for the chaos. "We're in rooms 113 and 114 down the corridor. Apparently the windows are small but serviceable."

"Mum?" I say in a small voice.

Mum holds out her arms. I hug her very tightly indeed.

We walk together down the corridor, dragging my suitcases with us.

"Not quite what you're used to, superstar," says Tina as we reach our new room. It is small and brown with a window the size of a postage stamp high up above our head.

I'm too tired and sad to rise to her teasing.

"It's perfect," I say, sitting down on the bed.

Mum and Dad settle Alex and Jake for the night in their room and then come over to ours for a family conference. Before Mum can get out her notebook or Dad can turn on the kettle in the corner of the room, I stand up.

"I want to say thank you for coming," I say nervously as they all look at me. "I don't deserve any of you and I'm so glad to see you. I'm an A-grade idiot."

"No arguments there," says Mum. "Thank you, Storm. It's been very difficult for all of us, and we appreciate the fact that you recognize that. It's all part of growing up, learning the difference between good and bad advice, and what it means to take responsibility for your choices."

I bite my lip. Dad takes the opportunity to flip the kettle switch.

"So now that Leo has got you out of Echo's clutches," says Mum in a brisker tone of voice, "do you have a plan B?"

I shake my head.

"Is it worth trying Sound Pacific again?" Dad asks.

"They'll never want to hear from me again," I say.

"Doesn't mean we shouldn't try," says Mum.

I smile wanly at her. *We* is my new favourite word.

"How's your famous boyfriend?" Tina asks me.

"He's not my boyfriend any more," I say with difficulty. "I don't think he ever was. He just kissed me once. He dumped me as soon as I told him I'd broken my deal with Echo."

"You're sure he dumped you?" Tina asks when I give her the sorry tale of him not taking my calls. "Even megastars can stumble into areas of bad reception."

"He unfollowed me on basically everything," I say. "If that's not a dumping, I don't know what is. He never liked me, Tina."

"If he kissed you, he must have liked you a bit," Tina points out.

I feel a faint stirring of hope. "Maybe," I say.

Tina pats me on the shoulder, which is about as comforting as my big sister ever gets. "He's probably moping about you somewhere, same as you're moping about him. Even megastars have feelings, Storm."

My sister, ever the romantic. I admit, her words do cheer me up a bit. Maybe I wasn't a complete waste of time in Jase's eyes. I pull up my Twitter feed to see if I can find any photos of him hanging around in dark glasses, looking soulfully out of windows or doing any of those things that can give clues on how a person might be feeling.

Very quickly, I wish I hadn't.

News 4 Youz @news4youz
.@jasem4real not wasting time w/o @stormhall_ official. @EchoMusicLtd's latest signing @meena2000 fixing his broken heart?

Celebrity News @celebnewsstories

.@jasem4real @meena2000 seen
@theclubattheivy sparking rumours of duet on
@EchoMusicLtd label

Meena @meena2000

Sooooo excited right now!!!!!!! @EchoMusicLtd
@jasem4real #worldtour

Elena Novak @qweenmahunny

JASE SHES NOT RIGHT FOR U I AM ALWAYS
HERE ♥♥♥

Tina tries to prise my phone from my lifeless
fingers as I stare at the picture of Jase posing with a
beautiful blonde girl in what I instantly recognize
as a Maleesh Clubwear dress. "Meena" has her hand
on the back of Jase's bristly red-dyed neck and Jase
has his hand on her neat little waist. The picture is
only about ten minutes old. Jase must have gone out
right after calling me this evening, and met this girl,
and . . . and. . .

Echo Music @EchoMusicLtd

.@jasem4real @meena2000 single BLUE
ANGEL out soon

Jase Mahone @jasem4real

@meena2000 can't wait to sing with U on tour xx

"There's no point staring at it," Tina says.

I resist Tina's fingers with all my might. They already have a single planned. It has a name and everything. It could have been me, duetting with Jase and touring the world. Instead it's Meena.

She's got my life now. And what have I got? Less than what I had before all this.

A big fat nothing.

CHAPTER 27

Bleak heart, lost soul, dead waste, no goal,
hopeless, hopeless, hopeless. . .

Yes. That's good. Definitely conveys the pit of despair I've been in for the past two days.

Bleee-ee-eak heart, weak heart, no strength
and no guts, no ifs and no buts, hopeless,
hopeless, ho-o-opeless. . .

I try sounding out a melody to match the words that are floating in my head but I'm shivering too much to hold the notes. Stretching out with my

263

toes, I turn the bath taps on. I've been in here for at least an hour, and have had to top it up three times. I'm wrinkly as a tortoise's neck but I don't care. I don't care about anything any more, except maybe this song.

Hopeless, ho-opeless, no way, no go, just crushed by this blow, bleak heart, ble-eak heart. . .

It sounds good in the bathroom acoustics. Mellow and sad. There's a catch in my voice that I'm not forcing. It's just there, and it suits the song.

Crushed, crushed by this blow.

Tina hammers on the door. "If you sing that one more time, I won't be responsible for my actions," she yells through the hinges. "That melody and those lyrics are making Radiohead sound cheerful."

I sink down into the cooling bathwater, let my hair wash around me. I feel like a drowned sailor or that lady in the painting who floats down a flowery river. My voice fills my head until I can't hear anything else.

No way and no go, too crushed by this blow, bleak heart, blea-eak heart.

"You can't stay in there for ever, Storm! Anyway, I need my toothbrush."

I try and tune Tina out. It's warm and safe in here and I can just float away with my thoughts. Why would I want to leave? There's nothing for me outside our hotel room.

I put on my headphones and crank up the volume, losing myself in Billie Holiday's mournful voice. Who needs social media, the news, the whirl of street life, the meetings, the auditions? All that stuff fills me with horror right now. I'm going to stay in this bath with Billie until the world has forgotten all about me. Or at least for as long as the water stays hot.

After another half hour, the water is running lukewarm and I have to admit defeat. I get slowly out of the bath and wrap myself in a towel straight off the heated towel rail. I reluctantly unlock the bathroom door.

Dad barrels straight into the bathroom shoulder-first.

"Bernie!" Mum cries as he smacks into the wall

opposite the door with an "Oof!" of surprise before slithering to a heap on the damp tiled floor. "I told you she must have been wearing her headphones. She was coming out, didn't you hear the bathwater draining from the tub?"

"What's everyone doing in here?" I ask as I slowly dry my ears.

"Tina was convinced that you were never coming out of this bathroom so she fetched your father – oh, Bernie, have you hurt yourself? – and he was going to knock the door down but then you opened it yourself and, oh, Storm. . ." Mum stops, wipes her forehead and, for once, looks totally lost for words.

"Bum," says Alex helpfully as Dad gets back on to his feet and wipes ineffectually at the wet marks all down his trousers.

I realize that my towel isn't covering me properly. I tug it into place. Jake and Alex collapse into giggles, which clash with the anxious looks I'm getting from everyone else.

"What?" I say. "Can't a person take a bath any more without getting in the fire brigade?"

"You were in there for hours," Tina says.

"It's not as if there's anything out here for me, is there?"

"There's always schoolwork to take your mind off things," Mum says. "Endrick are sending emails every day, giving you a chance to catch up."

I'd throw my hands in the air if it didn't mean letting go of my towel and setting my little brothers off again. "How is schoolwork supposed to help?" I demand. "Schoolwork is the LAST thing that's going to help!"

"You need to be prepared, Storm. In case we can't fix any more meetings, in case. . ."

"Please," I interrupt as tears brim in my eyes. "I need some space, OK? I'm fine, I'm out of the bathroom now, you don't need to fuss around me. Go somewhere, do something, I don't care, but please just GET OUT OF MY ROOM."

"It's my room too," Tina starts to say, but then she sees the look on my face and stops talking and shrugs and grabs her handbag and backs out of the room along with everyone else.

"You'll meet us for lunch, won't you?" says Mum. "You need to eat, love—"

I shut the door gently on her mid-sentence and lock the door. After casting a brief look of loathing at the Endrick emails cluttering up the screen on my laptop, I shut down my email and fire up FaceTime.

The only person I can face talking to right now is Belle. It's more than likely that she won't answer, but I have to try. And then maybe I'll think about putting some clothes on and joining my family for some food, on the *strict* understanding that no one mentions either singing or schoolwork or basically anything at all. In fact, I'm going to ask for complete silence.

If she answers.

If she doesn't, I'm getting back into the bath, lukewarm water or not.

I gaze blearily into my webcam. I look like some kind of swamp monster. A perfect reflection of how I'm feeling inside. Maybe if Belle sees me looking like this, she'll take pity on me and be my friend again. I have no one else.

It takes me a minute to realize that Colin Park is

peering at me down Belle's webcam. I yelp in shock and scoot back from the screen.

"Storm, is that you?" he asks.

"Colin," I squeak. "Um, I wasn't expecting you, I just got out of the bath."

He isn't supposed to see me like this. BELLE is supposed to see me like this. It's one thing having Belle taking pity on her swamp-monster ex-friend. It's something else entirely having her boyfriend doing the same thing.

Colin's face reminds me of a kindly pony as he peers at me through the long brown strands of his fringe. "Oh," he says. "Was it a nice bath?"

"Yes, I guess," I say, blushing like a hot lobster. "As baths go."

I frantically look around my desk for something handy to "accidentally" drop over the webcam.

"Bubbles?"

"No. Yes. Some," I say in desperation.

"I'm a shower guy myself."

I DON'T WANT TO KNOW THAT COLIN PARK IS A SHOWER GUY.

"Ah well," I say at last. "Each to their own."

"Belle likes baths," Colin continues. "I bought her some grapefruit bath gel last week. She smells fantastic now. Not that she didn't smell fantastic before, of course."

"That's so nice of you," I say, briefly diverted from the horror of this conversation by the cuteness of Colin buying Belle citrus-scented bath products. I didn't think guys knew about things like citrus-scented bath products. I bet Jase Mahone never bought anyone a citrus-scented bath product in his life.

I need to move this conversation away from "things really nice boyfriends do for their girlfriends" because otherwise I'm going to cry. I attempt to smooth my swampy hair away from my face while not getting my fingers too near the webcam. They redefine wrinkly.

"Is Belle there?" I ask.

"Yeah, she's downstairs, she should be up in a sec."

"Oh," I say awkwardly. "Um, so is everything

OK? Glasgow OK? Endrick OK? You OK? Belle OK?"

How many times am I going to use the word *OK*?

"Bonnie OK?" I add just because I HAVEN'T BROKEN THE WORLD RECORD FOR SAYING OK YET. "Jade OK, Sanjit OK, Daniel OK?"

"Yeah, everyone's fine, you know. Working hard, partying a bit, the usual stuff. How's London?"

"Great!!" I say in the brightest voice that I can muster. It practically kills me. Colin doesn't use social media much, clearly. "Brilliant! Couldn't be better! So is Belle, um, OK?"

"She's fine, really. Enjoying life as a legal adult and all that."

It takes me a moment to work out what Colin means. When I understand, a whole fresh layer of awfulness hits me like a ten-ton truck. I work through the dates with my fingers. Yesterday, my BF turned sixteen without me.

"Colin, you have to tell Belle how sorry I am for missing her birthday yesterday," I gasp, when I can breathe again. "Things have been unbelievably crazy here. Please please please tell her that I'll be back for the party on Saturday. I wouldn't miss it for anything." I *knew* there was something happening on Saturday, I would never forget THAT.

Colin scrunches up his face. "About that," he says.

"Tell me," I say eagerly. "I'll help, I'll do anything. What does she need?"

"She doesn't need anything. She kind of did for a while, but you were busy so we all helped and everything's arranged now."

I pounce. "She needed my help? When? She should have asked, she knows I would do anything—"

"She wanted to talk to you about it last week but she said you weren't listening, or you thought she was talking about a party you went to or something?"

I need to talk to you about the party.

A fresh gust of horror grips me. How could I have been so totally self-obsessed to think she wanted to talk to me about ME?

"I thought. . ." I stammer. "I thought she. . . Look, never mind, I blew it, I know that now, but I'm not going to blow Saturday, OK? Please tell her, Colin. You'll tell her, won't you?"

Colin looks steadily at me down the webcam. "Storm," he says, "I'm really sorry, but Belle doesn't want you at her party."

CHAPTER 28

"What?" I whisper.

"If I could change her mind, I would. But you know what Belle is like."

I do. I know very well indeed. I know almost every detail of her party too, because we've been planning it for years. The theme is going to be space age. There will be bowls of Starburst divided up into separate colours. The ice cubes in the drinks will be rocket-shaped and the music will be all our favourite tracks. And 1D won't be the guest act because Belle doesn't have enough cookies.

I swallow, hard.

"Well," I say in a voice that doesn't sound like

mine, "if she feels like that, then obviously I won't come."

Colin's kind brown eyes are anxious. "I really am sorry."

I can't even force a smile. I just silently end the call.

OMGOMGOMG.

There is no way back from this place.

I pace around my hotel room like a lion in a very tiny cage. Glasgow has never felt so far away as it does right now. I pace and I brood and I pace some more. I log on to Facebook and gaze hungrily at all the photos of Belle and everyone having fun without me. When I have seen enough pictures of Belle-without-me to make me scream, I switch to Instagram to do the same thing. Pace, brood, pace. Brood, pace, brood.

The only thing that stops me going totally mad is a glimpse of myself in the bathroom mirror. I have to do something about my hair before it fixes itself into all eternity, swamp monster style.

Twenty minutes later, dressed and dry (not

counting my tear-streaked face), I'm pacing again and making plans. I'll go to Glasgow. I'll get there on the next bus. I'll storm up to Belle's house on Saturday night in my fiercest outfit ever and I won't even ring the bell. Instead, I'll go round the back of the house and stand at the French windows like some kind of avenging fairy. I will wait until Belle sees me. The party will freeze, the music will stop. Belle will open the French windows. I will tell her how much she has hurt me by banning me from her party, and how betrayed I feel.

"How did our friendship come to this?" I will shout.

And then I will let her cry for a bit before forgiving her and going inside for the biggest make-up party of our lives.

I am so caught up in my fantasy that, mid-pace, I stub my toe hard on the bed leg. It KILLS and I have to sit down and breathe and try to get myself back to normal. But when I reach normal, I start crying again. Everything in my fantasy – every last dramatic scene, every screamed word of betrayal and every last millimetre of my epic, crowd-pleasing outfit – proves that Belle is right not to want to be my friend any more. I'm self-obsessed: tick. I'm a drama queen: tick. I don't respect her wishes: tick.

I need to scale this back to basics. Apologize and expect nothing in return. Belle deserves to have the party that she wants, with or without me. I'd prefer to stub my toe again rather than live for one more second with the mental pain of that thought.

Through the clattering of my brain, Mum knocks at the door.

"We're back, but we thought we'd take the boys to London Zoo," she says. "You want to come?"

Tough call. London Zoo, or sitting in here wallowing in the knowledge that Belle doesn't like me any more? My life already feels like the monkey enclosure at feeding time. I might as well see a few monkeys for real.

The day at the zoo is surprisingly fun, given that my heart has been smashed into itsy-bitsy pieces. We all buy animal masks in the shop to get us in the right mood. I choose a monkey mask. Dad pays extra for a zoo-themed thermos for his coffee and Mum looks dreamily at a scarf printed with parrots.

"Penguins!" Jake screams, pulling us all in one direction.

"Train!" Alex screams five minutes later, pulling us the other way.

Tina drops her leopard mask over her face every time she sees a boy that she fancies so she can check them out without them realizing. I stay behind my mask the whole time, only ever lifting it so that I can lick my ice cream without giving myself a beard. Today of all days, when my world has collapsed in ruins around me, I do NOT want to be recognized. The way I'm feeling right now, I wonder if I'll ever enjoy being recognized again.

"Selfie?" Tina suggests every now and again, as we wander among the enclosures and lose ourselves in all the weird jungly noises we can hear.

"I'll take one of you if you want," I say.

"Don't you want one of you too?"

I shake my head silently and eat more ice cream.

When it's feeding time for the penguins, I make an excuse about the stink of fish and sit outside with my phone, where I switch on Twitter and officially retire my @stormhall_official handle.

Storm Hall @stormhall_singer
It's all about the music #neverforget

I left Echo because they weren't about the music. This tweet feels right, whatever happens next. I go through the rest of my feeds and do the same thing. Each name change, each comment about the music gives me back a sense of power. Power that I lost for a while. Power I'm going to get back.

I may not have Belle in my life any more, but I can still have music.

CHAPTER 29

"Come on then," says Dad in my ear.

I sit up blearily and rub my eyes. Feel a rush of gladness that my parents are still here and I'm not in the hotel room upstairs, alone. Tina snores on in the bed beside me.

"Where are we going?"

"It's a surprise. Can you be ready in ten minutes?"

Ten minutes is a BIG ask. But true to my word – that I'm going to do things differently from now on – I take the quickest shower in the universe, apply the minimum level of make-up and sling on the first clothes that I see. The only time I slow down is when I'm selecting the right pair of sunglasses. Certain things cannot be rushed.

"Record time," says Dad in the reception hall. "We'll take a bus. There's a stop outside."

"Where are we going?" I ask, following him out into the street.

"I already told you," he says cryptically.

"No you didn't."

Dad ignores this. Instead, he takes my hand and helps me on board a freshly arrived bus. "Written any new songs lately?" he asks as he waves two travel cards at the driver.

I tell him about Belle's song, the one I wrote in the hotel last week. The one I thought, stupidly, that Echo Music might be interested in hearing. I sing him the lyrics up in the top of the bus. We're the only ones up there, and the acoustics are quite good.

"Great," Dad says. "We'll start with that."

My father is being extra maddening today.

"Dad," I say, "I still have no idea what you're on about."

He does his cryptic grin again. "Any other new material to show me?"

I sing a few words of my Radiohead-is-cheerful number. Where is he going with this?

"Let's just stick with the first one for today," he says diplomatically as the bus stops with a wheeze. "This is our stop, I think."

We get off the bus. I stare at the big glass door set in the front of a posh white building beside the bus stop. *Hazelnut Studios*, says a steel plaque set into the wall. *You bring the music, we'll crack the rest.*

"See?" says Dad gleefully. "I told you after all. Record time. Re*cord* time!"

He's looking so pleased with himself that I actually laugh for the first time in what feels like ages. "That's so bad, it's almost good," I tell him.

"The best thing to do after falling off a horse," says Dad, guiding me through the glass door, "is to put the headphones back on. In a manner of speaking. I've booked us two hours and a session musician. Rory's come down for this too. Let's see if we can bring back your mojo, eh?"

My first thought on entering the studio is how peaceful it feels. The recording room looks surprisingly similar to the one at Spacebar Studios. Then Dad's friend Rory begins the beat on the bongos, picking out a few funky rhythms. I pick up a set of headphones and swing them on my fingers. The last time I wore a pair of these was one of the worst days of my life. This could be a fresh start, right?

Rory keeps the rhythm going as Steve the guitarist nods his head along to the beat. The room fills with a thoughtful, pulsing sound that suits the track perfectly. Taking my cue from their cute air of professionalism, I sing my heart out, filling the song with all the pain I'm feeling for Belle right now. My voice sounds completely different, even to my own ears: older, wiser and deeper. I lean into the mic and give it everything I've got.

Hey
I got a little story to say
About looking up and changing your way
As time is passing you by

Laugh
I'm gonna make you look and laugh
I'm gonna make you appreciate
Life is all we have

Steve the guitarist anticipates my every move, bending the sound of the guitar around my words. Dad smiles at me through the glass partition.

Give yourself a little, time time time time time

We use the full two hours to make it as good as we can. And when we finish, Steve the guitarist shakes our hands and asks if he can work with us again sometime. Exhausted, I collapse on the sofa beside Dad and rest my head on his shoulder. We sit there in Hazelnut Studios' green room for a while, enjoying the feeling.

"I needed that," I say.

Dad pats my hand. "I know."

"It's not going to be any use, though," I add sadly. "Is it?"

"The Storm I know doesn't give up like this."

"Welcome to the new Storm," I say. And I make a face.

"I prefer the old one," Dad says. "Storm, the answer to this is very simple. Try Sound Pacific again."

I allow myself a glimmer of hope, like a dieter allows themselves to sniff a chocolate bar. Then I wrap the chocolate bar up again.

"They wouldn't even let me through the doors," I point out. "I dumped all over them a couple of weeks ago, or have you forgotten?"

"As with so much in life," Dad says, "a fresh start can often begin with a simple apology. You need to apologize to Sound Pacific. It's obvious to me that you regret your actions. You can convince them too. And you have to play them this track. You owe it to yourself and to everyone who believes in you."

I feel ill at the thought of seeing Enrique Diablo again. Henry will definitely be the Devil today. He'll be horrible to me if I see him again, I know he will.

"There has to be someone else in London who would give me a chance," I say.

"With your track record? Not very likely, at least not at the moment," says Dad. "Put your ego behind you and face reality. Sound Pacific are your best chance. And if they don't take you back, we'll just go home, take some time and reassess the whole situation."

I take a deeeeeeeep breath. I had wanted things to be different from now on. Going back to Sound Pacific doesn't feel different. It feels like treading the same disastrous path as before. But even as I think this, I know I'm just making excuses.

"Tell it like it is, why don't you?" I say to buy myself a little time.

Dad looks at me steadily over the rim of his coffee mug as I chew my lip, trying not to think too hard about what I need to do. It's going to be awful and my gut clenches just thinking about it. But Dad's right. What choice do I have?

"Fine," I sigh. "I'll give it a try. But only to shut you up."

CHAPTER 30

Mum fluttered round me like an anxious butterfly at breakfast this morning, straightening my jacket and fussing with my hair. "Are you sure you don't want me and Dad to come in with you?" she said again and again. "Really sure?"

More than anything, I want my parents with me now as I stand outside the Sound Pacific Records building. I want to feel my mother's hand in mine and I want to smell the coffee wafting from Dad's eternal travel mug. But I told them to take Jake and Alex to Hamleys today and let Tina go shopping by herself for once. I wouldn't take no for an answer.

I made this mess, and it's up to me to get out of it. Only I can't seem to move.

Ping.

> Thx for stepping in this morning, sis. Already found this. You can borrow it maybe in five years when Im bored of wearing it. You in yet?

I study the picture of the dress my sister's just texted me. It's gorgeous. I wish I were shopping with her instead of standing here shaking like a leaf.

> Still on pavement outside. Dont think I can do this L

> U can borrow in TWO years if you get in there, best offer UR gonna get

Sliding my phone into my pocket, I practise breathing for a few minutes. I've come this far. All I have to do is go through those doors and...

"Hi. Could I speak to Mr Diablo?"

I steady the palms of my hands on the cool marble top of the reception desk and maintain eye contact with the reception lady.

"Do you have an appointment?"

"No, but it's Storm Hall and I want to tell Mr Diablo—"

"I'm sorry, but if you don't have an appointment, you can't see Mr Diablo."

"I just need him to hear something, it won't take long."

The receptionist's eyes flicker. I think she's just recognized me. Is that a good thing or a bad thing? Probably a bad thing.

"As I said," she repeats with a steely look, "if you don't have an appointment, I'm afraid Mr Diablo can't see you. He is fully booked today. If you would like to call and arrange an appointment—"

My poise, what there is of it anyway, collapses. "Please," I say, with one of those embarrassing hiccups you get when you're terrified. "It's so important."

"I can give you his secretary's email," says the receptionist.

I can tell that this is the best I'm going to get.

"OK," I whisper, swallowing. "I'll take that, thanks. But can I wait? You know, in case Mr Diablo comes past?"

"You will be waiting a long time, Miss Hall. And Mr Diablo isn't famous for welcoming random enquiries in reception."

Ouch. I take it on the chin, though, as she scribbles down Mr Diablo's secretary's email. What else can I do? Then I go and sit on the waiting sofas. Where, surprise surprise, I wait.

Celebrity News @celebnewsstories
New tour dates announced. @jasem4real with special guest star @meena2000 #reddevil #berlin

Maleesh Clubwear @maleesh
Hot to trot, @meena2000 in S/S17 #fashion #fomo

New 4 Youz @news4youz
>>>NEWS EGGSCLUSIVE<<< @jasem4real fan
scores bullseye with @meena2000

I look at the scribbled email address the reception lady has given me. It has to be worth a try, right? If he listens to it?

slupitski@SoundPacific.com
Dear Ms Lupitski,
I would be grateful if you could play the attached
sound file to Mr Diablo. He knows good music
when he hears it, so I'm hoping this song will
show him how sorry I am about the mess that I
have caused.
Yours sincerely,
Storm Hall

I upload the recording we made at Hazelnut Studios and press send before I lose my nerve. In a moment of inspiration, I email the song to Belle as well. It can't hurt to show her that I'm thinking of her.

Then I wait some more.

Make it 1 year, you drive a hard bargain GET IN
THERE!!!

Bum bum bum HAHAHAHA

Storm, please ignore last, Alex got hold of my
phone. Hope things are going OK. Please tell us
if we can help. Love Mum xx

Time passes in a kind of haze. I start seeing the
same people moving back and forth around the
reception area, and they look at me with their own
little flashes of recognition.

I wait and I wait and I wait.

"Miss Hall."

I look up from checking my phone and feel all the
blood leave my body. Enrique Diablo is standing in
reception looking at me with eyes as hard and brown
as pebbles. I jump to my feet. My knees buckle
sideways as pins and needles flood through me.

"Emma on reception tells me that you have been here for three and a half hours," he says.

That explains the pins and needles. "I know you don't want to see me or waste your time with me any more but I just wanted to say sorry for wasting your time and missing my big chance," I say hurriedly, before he can walk away and I lose him for ever. "Echo was a massive mistake, I know that now. I don't know what came over me when I signed with them and not with you after you were so kind and said such lovely things about my singing. And, um, that's all."

"You just wanted to say sorry," he repeats. "So the song you sent to my secretary you did for fun, hmm?"

I flush. "Well, I wanted to say sorry but, yes, I also thought I would play you my new song because I hoped that even if you didn't see me in person you would maybe hear the song and know I'm sorry that way too. Because . . . because I am."

Slick, Storm, I think hopelessly as Enrique Diablo checks his watch. *Really cool*. This is even worse than I thought it would be.

"So . . . you heard the song?" I say desperately.

"I heard it," he confirms.

Tears blur my eyes. There's no way he is going to give me a second chance. "I understand that you're angry," I say. "I don't deserve even this conversation."

"This much is true," he agrees.

I look at him in a sort of agonized daze. "Was my song any good?"

"I don't have to answer that."

My heart sinks as he moves away from me towards the lift. He's leaving. He isn't interested.

"No," I say in a voice that sounds so broken, I hardly recognize it. "You don't. Thank you for your time. I'll go now."

I pick up my bag, fighting back the tears, looking at the marble floor of Sound Pacific's reception area like my life depends on it.

"I'll go now," I repeat quietly.

"Why did you think a song would work as an apology, Miss Storm?"

I force myself to look up at his unsmiling face. "I would have apologized in person but I couldn't get in to see you. The song was the only thing that I had left."

He stares at me very hard. "Did you really think I would take you back? After everything that you did? I was left in a very embarrassing position. The executives were very disappointed in your behaviour, and so was I."

The last faint flicker of hope dies inside me. I feel strangely calm.

"I wish I could change what's happened, but I can't, and I understand completely how you feel," I say. "If I were you, I wouldn't give me a second chance either."

He nods at this. "So what are you going to do now?"

"Go home, I suppose," I say dully. "Get on with my life."

"Your song, by the way," he says. "It was good."

Tears drip from the end of my nose. "Thank you. I'm glad you liked it."

I wait for him to dismiss me, or call security to escort me from the building. Instead, he says something extraordinary.

"I have a board meeting in five minutes. I will play them your track. I'll tell them you are a new talent and that you sound a bit like Storm Hall. If they don't like it, then you can go home and no one needs to know that we did this. If they do like it, then we may have an interesting problem."

I feel as if I've slipped into a parallel universe. "You'd do that?" I say in disbelief. "After . . . after everything?"

He gives a very brief flick of a smile. "I hate to see talent go to waste. You have blotted your copybook and the board would most likely never consider you again. But your music, perhaps, is a different matter."

I have to keep control. I can't blub or scream. I can't even smile. This is more than I could have hoped for.

"Please," I say. "Can I wait and hear what they say?"

Mr Diablo is moving towards the lifts.

"I hardly think I can stop you, Miss Hall," he says briskly.

CHAPTER 31

I burst into the hotel's reception like a tornado.

"They liked it!" I shout. "They liked it, they liked it! And now they want to hear it live tomorrow!"

My entire family – Mum, Dad, Tina and what feels like about a hundred Jakes and Alexes – fall on top of me in a shouty, squealy sort of heap. Some of the more proper London types eating their cream teas in the window of the reception narrow their eyes at the noise. One old gentleman drops a blob of clotted cream on the tablecloth instead of on his scone.

"Oh my goodness," says Mum in excitement. "Oh my goodness me."

"Storm, oh Storm," weeps Dad, kissing the top of my head.

"I GOT A TRICERATOPS FROM HAMLEYS," says Alex.

"You're so jammy," Tina says, giving me a squeeze.

"ALEX FARTED ON THE BUS," says Jake.

When we have all calmed down, I explain everything. The board liked my song. They believed Mr Diablo's line and thought that I was someone else. I told him that I felt like a different singer now – softer round the edges, darker and more thoughtful – and it was obviously showing in my music. It would show in my behaviour too, I said. He would see for himself.

"Oh my goodness," says Mum for about the hundredth time. "They want to hear you live tomorrow?"

"How are you going to sing live for this board tomorrow when they all hate your guts?" asks Tina, cutting to the heart of the problem still facing me.

The thought of revealing my true identity has

been giving me palpitations ever since Mr Diablo gave me the extraordinary news earlier. I literally have NO idea how I'm going to do this. But I'm flying like a kite right now because they *like my music*. If they like my music, they'll like me again. They *have* to.

"I'll figure something out," I say.

"You can sing in my penguin mask from London Zoo if you like," Jake offers.

I ruffle Jake's hair. "Cheers, Jakey. I might take you up on that."

"Have you told Belle?" asks Tina.

My brilliant mood dips faster than a seagull diving for a chip. I haven't had a response from my email yet, the one where I sent Belle her song.

"I don't think she wants to know," I say.

Mum rubs my back. "Of course she'll want to know, love. She's your best friend!"

"*Was* my best friend. Isn't my best friend any more."

"All friends argue," Dad says.

"It's not about an argument. It's about me not

being there for Belle when she needed me. I forgot to call her on her sixteenth birthday. And. . ." This is still very hard to say, even after everything else that has happened today. ". . . and she's told me she doesn't want me to come to her birthday party this weekend."

Everyone is silent. A world where I'm not friends with Belle Monaghan Pace is unthinkable, for my family as well as for me.

"I still think you should tell her about Sound Pacific," says Tina at last. "It'll only make things worse if she finds out from someone else."

"I can't call her," I say. "I can't take her slapping me down again."

"You give up too easily," says Tina impatiently. "Message her if you don't want to call."

Tina's right, I suppose. I decide to break the news via a direct message on Facebook. Personal, but not too personal. Belle wants to keep me at arm's length right now, and I have to respect that.

I scroll through my contacts to find her name. Scroll again.

This isn't possible. But there it is, in blue and white. Or, to be more accurate, NOT in blue and white.

Belle has unfriended me.

It takes two strawberry tarts at the café over the road from the hotel before I can stop crying. Mum and Dad give up trying to calm me down after one, and take the boys off somewhere for the rest of the afternoon. Tina is still hanging in there, silently handing me tissues – well, serviettes from the table dispenser – every time I wail, "But it CAN'T be true, Belle would never do that, I haven't been THAT bad, have I?" Which I do quite a lot.

After twenty minutes, I grope blindly for another serviette, but the dispenser is empty.

"They're finished," says my sister. "And you look awful."

Tina has never been into the playing-nice side of being a sister. It's good for me, mostly.

"Tina," I say, sniffing, "what am I going to do?"

"About Belle, or about Sound Pacific?"

I rest my head on the table. The ironic thing here is that Belle would know what to do right now.

"Both," I say in a muffled voice.

Tina finishes off my tart. "How about," she suggests through the crumbs, "we worry about Sound Pacific first, and then get back to worrying about Belle after you've sung for the board?"

That's logical, I suppose. Belle is in Glasgow, whereas the Sound Pacific board is a twenty-minute taxi ride away. They want to hear me at ten o'clock tomorrow morning while Belle never wants to hear from me again.

"I can't believe I have to face that board tomorrow and say, 'Remember me, the one who dumped on you last time? Well, I'm back!'" I groan. "What if they kick me right out again?"

Tina waves her hand like my words are an annoying fly buzzing round our heads, hardly worth a second of our attention. "You have Mr Diablo on your side. They'll have to get past him first. And of course, there's the outfit."

I rub my eyes. "What outfit?"

"The outfit that is going to say to these guys tomorrow, I'm the new Storm Hall and I'm going to rock your world before you throw me out of here." Tina stands up and shoulders her bag. "Come on, wimp. We're going shopping."

Within ten minutes – and a top-speed repair job on my make-up – we are out of the café and on a mission to find an outfit that will say everything I need it to say. Strong, independent, soulful, marketable and majorly fabulous. Plus, of course, not afraid to stand up in front of a load of people who are going to hate that I'm back. That's a LOT of message from one outfit. We have our work cut out. But we're the Hall sisters and retail challenges hold no fear for us. We can do this.

Like Tina says, I should only worry about one thing at a time.

CHAPTER 32

"There will be five people in the room. Myself and those board members that you met last time. And your session musicians, of course. Guitar and bongos, yes?"

I picture the four people sitting in the window of Mr Diablo's office last time I was in there. I can't remember anything about them at all, except that they were sitting very still the whole time. My knees are shaking. I clasp my hands tightly together and keep my eyes on Mr Diablo's face.

"Do you remember their names?" he says.

I shake my head. I can barely remember my own name right now. The outfit that Tina and I found yesterday, the structured yellow jacket and the close-fitting cropped trousers, feels like a comforting exoskeleton. Without them I would be a puddle on the floor round about now.

Mr Diablo goes through the names one by one. "John Shelley, chief executive officer of Sound Pacific, and the most important man in the room. He will be wearing a black suit – he always wears black – and he will be the most difficult to persuade."

"He liked the song, right?"

Mr Diablo doesn't crack a smile. "Yes," he says. "That is your winning card and you must play it like your life depends on it."

"It does, Mr Diablo," I say fervently.

"Lindsay Littleton. Chief financial officer. She was the one who was least convinced by your song when I played it to her yesterday. It will take very little to prove to her that you are wrong for Sound Pacific and we should not give you another chance. She will be wearing very bright lipstick and, if you're asked to sing more afterwards, she'll probably be looking out of the window as you sing. This doesn't necessarily mean that she doesn't like you. It simply means that she is weighing the risk of taking on a new artist against the profits that the artist could make for Sound Pacific."

Sheesh. This guy really knows how to give a pep talk.

"John Shelley, CEO," I repeat. "Lindsay Littleton, CFO."

"Cameron Conaway. Chief marketing officer. He will talk too much but underneath his brain is like a machine. He can sell anything but he is very particular."

I picture Cameron Conaway like a market trader in a pork-pie hat, flogging mouldy bananas. I'm the mouldy bananas in this scenario.

"Finally," says Mr Diablo, gazing at me over the tips of his steepled fingers, "we will have Amanda Fairchild. Head of legal and commercial affairs. Mind like a razor, tongue even sharper."

"Mouldy bananas, Amanda Fairchild," I repeat.

Mr Diablo looks at me strangely.

"I mean, Cameron Conaway. And they're in the room already? Waiting?"

When he nods at this, I ask the question that has been bothering me since he gave me this lifeline yesterday.

"So, the minute I walk in – won't they just refuse to listen to me sing?"

"They'll be sitting with their backs to the stage and judging you purely on the sound of your voice. I have given them to understand, in very general terms, that your appearance has something curious about it and I do not wish them to be influenced by what they see."

"But what if they look anyway?"

"They will of course try," he says. "But I have thought of that."

I am reminded of Jake's offer of his penguin mask.

"What are you going to do?" I ask nervously.

"I have placed a screen on the stage," he says, looking pleased with himself. "You will stand behind that screen."

I want to hide my face behind my hands. Then

I remember all the time Tina spent getting my make-up right this morning and I resist because I do not want to smear what she has done to my eyelids. I curl my hands by my sides instead, digging my deep red fingernails into my palms.

"This is very important," says Mr Diablo, as if I haven't worked this out for myself. "These people are the ones who control the purse strings and they will have the final say on this matter. If they say no, there is nothing more that I can do for you."

"I understand," I say. I feel a bit breathless and hope that I can control my singing when it starts. "I'm so grateful for this chance, Mr Diablo."

His face softens a little. Not much, mind. More like how a rock softens when it's got a bit of lichen on it.

"A great deal depends on your performance, Storm, because it is not only your reputation that you are trying to save today," he reminds me. His eyes glint. "It is mine as well. Perform to the best of your ability. Prove to them that you were not a mistake the first time round. Prove to them that my faith is not unfounded."

I nod.

"My assistant will fetch you in five minutes."

He leaves this little room and shuts the door quietly behind him.

I want to sit down but there is only one hard chair in the corner and I'm afraid that if I sit down I'll never be able to get up again. So I stay upright, and I pace around for a bit, and I go through the lyrics of "Time" in my head. I tell myself that I mustn't think about Belle when I sing it. And then I change my mind, and tell myself the opposite. I wrote it for Belle, because I love her and I miss her, so of course I must think of her when I sing it. Being true to the feeling is the only way I'm going to get through this.

I think of my family waiting anxiously at the coffee shop five minutes' walk from here, the place Dad found the first time that I sang for Sound Pacific. I check my phone, making sure that everything is switched off. I don't check for messages. If there's still nothing from Belle, my heart really will break and I won't be able to sing at all.

There is a soft knock.

"They are ready for you, Miss Hall."

I walk down the softly carpeted corridor after Mr Diablo's assistant. I am shown a door, and when it opens, I find myself behind the little stage where I sang last time. True to his word, Mr Diablo has erected a screen between me and the board. I picture them all sitting exactly where they sat last time, by the window, coffees in their hands.

I exchange a nervous smile with the session musicians. I recognize the guitarist from last time. He recognizes me too with a little start of surprise, his fingers poised on his strings.

I don't think the board has realized that I've come in yet. I can hear them talking.

"I don't like this mystery, Enrique. It suggests to me that you have something to hide."

"Relax and enjoy it, John."

John Shelley. CEO. Difficult to persuade. Other voices murmur: a talkative one that I guess is

Cameron Conaway, and a woman.

"If this secrecy means you're giving me a legal issue to unravel here, Enrique, I won't thank you."

Amanda Fairchild, I think. Head of legal and commercial affairs.

"Trust me, Amanda," says Mr Diablo, confirming my suspicions. "There is no legal problem."

"I'm looking forward to it," says Cameron Conaway cheerfully. "It's like that show, *The Voice*. Which is a *supreme* piece of staging, I have to say. What a hook, spinning chairs to decide your fate. Why don't we have the chairs? I want the chairs."

"Do be quiet, Cameron," says a light voice. The kind of voice that wears bright lipstick, I think. Lindsay Littleton, CFO.

"I bet she's tied in with someone else," Amanda Fairchild repeats grimly.

Mr Diablo claps his hands. "When you are ready?" he says.

It's our cue.

The board members fall silent. I picture them trying to winkle through the screen with their beady eyes, wondering who's back here. I smooth down my jacket and nod at the guitarist and the bongo player.

This is for you, Belle.

"Hey
I got a little story to say
About looking up and changing your way. . ."

I sing through the catch in my voice. I don't think I'm going to make it through the catch in my voice, but I do. I think it improves the sound, maybe. Makes it richer, gives it an extra layer. Please forgive me, Belle. Please be my friend again.

"You gotta stop and feel the love
Gotta hold on to what you got
Never give it up. . ."

We used to jump off the swings at the same time, me and Belle. We would fly so high, trying to outswing each other, and then we would take off like birds. We usually fell over and grazed our knees but we laughed through the pain and we knew that we would be friends for ever. Thought we knew, anyway.

> *"We're so pressured to be bigger, better, braver*
> *When you are your own saviour*
> *Give yourself a little time. . ."*

There are real tears on my face as I sing the final words. The session guys both have their eyes closed. The bongos fade. The guitar player's head remains bent over the strings, playing the notes until there is nothing but the highest, gentlest plucking of strings, which hangs for a moment in the air like a rainbow and then goes away.

There is absolute silence on the other side of the screen. I clasp my hands tightly and wait to hear my fate.

Then I hear the gorgeous sound of one person applauding. Another person joins in, then another. They are murmuring things like "special" and "extraordinary" at each other. I can't quite tell if everyone is clapping. I suspect John Shelley isn't; I can feel it.

"Come out," I hear him say. "Whoever you are."

CHAPTER 33

I move towards the edge of the screen like a condemned criminal walking to the chopping block. The guitarist meets my eye and grimaces. He knows what happened first time round. He recognizes how difficult this is going to be.

"First, your opinion," Mr Diablo says, staying my execution.

John Shelley gives an exclamation of impatience. "You've played your games, Enrique. Let's see her. Out you come, miss."

I step out from behind the screen.

I remember them all now that I can see them. John Shelley in his black suit. Cameron Conaway without a pork-pie hat, but with a large pair of heavy-framed spectacles on his snubby nose. Amanda Fairchild with high hair and higher shoes. Lindsay Littleton in her bright lippy – pink today, red last time – looking fixedly out of the window. I stand there like a rabbit caught in someone's headlights.

The CEO's face is as white as a sheet. Without taking his eyes off me, he marches towards the sound equipment lining the side of the office. He flips the switch off. I feel the mic go dead in my hand.

"Is that. . ." says Cameron Conaway.

"That's. . ." says Amanda Fairchild.

Lindsay Littleton continues to look out of the window. "Oh, sure, *sounds* like Storm Hall," she murmurs to herself.

"Enrique," John Shelley growls. "What the *hell* are you playing at?"

"You have to admit, John," Mr Diablo says, "that she sang very well."

John Shelley comes closer. His eyes scorch me like fire, but the rest of his face remains composed.

"You've got a lot of nerve coming back here," he says.

I am completely terrified, but I stand my ground. "Mr Diablo invited me back," I say. "To give me a chance to apologize to you all and to show you that I have learned my lesson and grown into the kind of artist that Sound Pacific would be proud to represent."

"Proud?" John Shelley echoes. "We made you an offer and you threw it back in our faces and then proceeded to mock us in the media! And what did we ever do to deserve that? Do you have any idea how lucky you were to get that break in the first place?"

I must not cry. I WILL not cry.

"That tweet was not what it seemed, and I deleted it as soon as I realized people were taking it the wrong way. It was stupid of me and I apologize," I say as calmly as I can. "Echo made hay of it, but that was never my intent. I deeply regret turning down your offer. I'm so grateful to have had this second chance to sing for you all.

And even if you don't want to take me back, then at least I can hold my head up and tell myself that I tried."

John Shelley still doesn't look happy. Mr Diablo, on the other hand, looks delighted. I get the feeling that he's enjoying this.

"I think you liked the song," I say, "or you wouldn't have wanted to hear me live. I hope . . . you liked it enough to look past everything that's happened."

"She's rather adorable," murmurs Cameron Conaway.

Amanda Fairchild gives him a withering look. Then she fixes on me. "You signed with Echo," she says.

"I've broken with them now," I say quickly. "My lawyer found a problem with the contract."

"Sounds about right," snorts the head of legal and commercial affairs. "Echo couldn't write a contract if their lives depended on it."

"Give us one good reason why we should take you back," says John Shelley.

This is where I cannot fail. I have to prove here and now that I'm over my childish days and ways and ready to be a hard-working, responsible adult. If I can show that not even a scary CEO in a black suit can shoot me down, then anything is possible.

I lift my chin.

"You like my music," I say. "I know you don't like me personally and I understand why, but you're a record company, not ... not a person company. Although I'm not that bad really," I add, as an afterthought. "I'm just a bit stupid sometimes."

Cameron Conaway snorts with laughter. John Shelley silences him with a look.

"Can I have a word, John?" Lindsay Littleton has looked away from the window at last, and is beckoning the CEO over. John Shelley joins her and the other two in the window for a murmured conversation while Mr Diablo stays by the door, fiddling with his cufflinks. I stand very tall and do my best not to bite off all my lipstick. I'd give anything to hear what they're saying.

The CEO turns back to me.

"Please come here, young lady," he says.

Making my way down from the stage, I feel as if I'm stepping off a scaffold. MUST. NOT. SHOW. FEAR.

John Shelley studies me for a long, hard, eternal moment.

Then he smiles.

"This wouldn't be rock 'n' roll if we didn't give true talent a second chance," he says. "Welcome back."

Something erupts inside me. It takes every ounce of willpower not to scream for joy. But that's what a kid does and I am now an adult.

An adult with a recording contract.

A REAL RECORDING CONTRACT.

"Thank you so much," I croak. "I won't let you down. I'll never let you down again."

"Make it count, Miss Hall," says Mr Diablo when it's his turn to shake my hand.

"I will." My face is practically cracking with happiness. "I promise."

He looks thoughtfully at me. "And the regrets

that you were singing about. They are all sorted now, yes?"

I flush bright red. "Some of them," I say.

He smiles. "Well, I hope you're able to sort out the rest."

CHAPTER 34

I'm too excited to take the lift down. I feel like I could fly from the top-floor windows. But I'm not completely insane, so I take the stairs instead, winging down them three or four at a time, swinging round the corners with my hands on the banisters and my feet in the air. Every part of me feels like it's been put through a tumble dryer and has come out again slightly the wrong shape. I've done it. Sound Pacific want me back. I have a contract with the greatest record label in the world. Even if Jase Mahone is waiting for me at the bottom of these stairs with a bag of diamonds and the promise of a world tour, I won't let this miracle slip through my fingers again.

As I step outside, I'm surprised the whole world isn't sprinkled in rainbows and fairy dust. It looks just the same as it did when I went into Sound Pacific this morning. Grey and a bit grubby, but somehow a whole lot more wonderful.

Call your lawyer, Amanda Fairchild told me. *Make sure this is the deal that you really want this time.*

We'll put together big plans for you. Cameron Conaway. *Very big plans indeed.*

I stand by the side of the road for a while, just . . . existing. Being part of the pavement, and the air, and the flutter of pigeon wings. Every little thing feels magical. I am determined to savour it all.

On the bus stop, there is a large poster of Meena and Jase posing, arms draped around each other. TWO POP SENSATIONS, TOGETHER IN CONCERT! says the headline. There is a splatter of broken eggshell on Meena's face.

"Good luck, Meena," I tell her pretty, pouting face. "You're going to need it."

I have so many song ideas tumbling around in my head. It's as if my re-audition for Sound Pacific has unlocked a secret door in my mind that's full of bass drops, hooks and lyrics all longing to burst out on the world. I'm going to write songs about all the good things in life, and a few of the bad things too. I'm going to give Sound Pacific the album of their lives.

I skip across a zebra crossing, waving at all the other pedestrians as I go. They clearly think that I'm mad, but I don't care. I snap a picture of myself halfway across, winking at the camera.

Storm Hall @stormhall_singer
Can't wait to share my music with the world.
#music

I won't say anything else until I have that signed contract in my hands. I'm not risking a single thing with this incredible second chance that I've been given. Keep the fans guessing, I say.

Storm Hall @stormhall_singer
Hey @qweenmahunny. When life gives U broken

eggs, make an omelette! #love #happiness
#music

"Are you that girl who dated Jase Mahone?" says someone as I prance along the pavement, humming under my breath.

"No," I say cheerfully. "You're mixing me up with someone else. Someone who is looooong gone. Have a great day!"

Hop, skip, jump across the flagstones, avoiding the cracks like I used to when I was eight years old.

"Storm! Can I have a selfie?"

I blow them a kiss instead and dance on down the road.

News 4 Youz @news4youz
.@stormhall_singer seen behaving strangely
near offices of @SoundPacific, setting tongues
wagging, more when we have it #musicnews
#gossip

Celebrity News @celebnewsstories

New deal for @stormhall_singer in the wind?

sniffs the air #musicnews

Meena @meena2000

Loving my new #maleeshclubwear, foxeeee!!!!

@maleesh @EchoMusicLtd

I'm getting a bit breathless with all this dancing
so I slow down a bit and lean against a shop window
for a breather. The jacket in the display reminds me
of the awesome jacket Belle and I saw in the mall
together. How is it possible to feel sad and delighted
all at the same time? It's a very weird combination.

I will sort this out with Belle, I vow to myself.
I don't care how long it takes. I will show her, just
like I showed Sound Pacific, that I'm worth another
chance.

When I reach the coffee shop where my family
is waiting, I adjust my expression and try to look a
bit more serious. Where's the fun in sharing news
when your face is giving it away?

Mum stands up so quickly when she sees me come in that her chair falls backwards and lands on Dad's foot. Dad shouts. Alex drops his dinosaur in Tina's mochaccino, and Tina yells at him about putting his disgusting fingers all over her hot beverage. There is such chaos that I stand back for a bit and wait for things to settle down to normal again. Honestly, you can't take this family ANYWHERE.

Finally, Dad pulls out a chair and I sit down with what I hope is a totally neutral face.

"I went in and sang for them," I say. I look steadily round the table. "But unfortunately. . ."

"I knew it," Mum says in despair.

Dad puts a hand on Mum's arm, his eyes never leaving my face. "Steady on, Megs," he says. "Storm hasn't finished."

Alex takes his chance to fish his dinosaur out of Tina's drink while everyone else's attention is fixed on me.

"*Unfortunately*," I continue, relishing the way everyone's looking at me, "they liked me. They've made me another offer, and I'm going to accept it. Subject to Mum and Leo reading the contract this time, of course." If there's only one thing I learned from the Echo debacle, it's this: don't sign *anything* without your manager and your lawyer on hand.

If there was chaos before, it's nothing compared to the riot that now breaks out around our table. There are shouts and tears, and photographs and hugs, and shouts and more hugs. I think I am happier than I have ever been in my entire life. And do you know why? Not because of the record deal – although, obviously, that is incredibly wonderful and important – but because I'm here with my family, celebrating this wonderful and important thing.

"Can anyone join in the party?" says a familiar voice.

This time, it's MY turn to jump up so fast that I knock over my chair. Belle and Colin are standing in the coffee shop doorway.

"What are you doing here?" I gasp.

"Oh, you know," she says, smiling slightly. "Glasgow and London are pretty close together when you think about it."

I feel like I haven't seen Belle for *ages*. I gaze at her and she gazes back.

"I think it's time everyone had another croissant," says Dad. He takes Jake and Alex by their unprotesting hands and leads them to the pastry counter.

"I need another mocha," says Tina, going after them.

"And I need a wee," says Colin. "Except you probably didn't need to know that?"

Mum gets extremely busy on her phone, half turning her shoulder towards Belle and me as Colin slides away towards the toilets.

"You unfriended me," I say quietly.

"You were an idiot," Belle replies.

I nod. No arguments there.

"I got your song yesterday," says Belle. "Did you write it about me?"

I nod again, biting my lip.

"No one's ever written a song about me before."

"It was the best way I could think of to say sorry. You know, apart from actually talking to you."

The next minute I can feel her in my arms, her curls squished up against my wet and teary face.

"I've missed you so much," I sob into her hair. "I'm so sorry. I promise I'll never take you for granted again."

"It's OK, you big doughnut," says Belle as she rubs my back. "You great soppy twonk."

"BELLE AND STORM ARE KISSING," Alex announces to the coffee shop.

"We're friends again," I say, drying my eyes on a serviette. Serviettes have done me well in the crying department lately.

"Coffees are on me!" Dad exclaims.

"I can't believe you came all the way to London to see me," I say, sinking down at our table again. I am holding tightly on to Belle's hand in case she runs out into the street and out of my life again.

Belle and Colin exchange a look. It's a look I've been missing for months. It's the "Storm always thinks it's about her" look.

"You didn't come to London for me at all, did you?" I say.

"We came to this *coffee shop* for you," Belle says, squeezing my hand. "But *London* – not exactly. We were in town when Tina called, so that's why we're here now."

I swing round to look at Tina. "You called them?"

"I told you not to give up," my sister says with a shrug. "But you weren't listening."

I take Belle's hand again. "I'm just really, really pleased to see you."

"Why are you in London?" Mum asks.

I'm really glad she asked that. That was going to be my next question. Because I'm actually dying of curiosity now. If they aren't in London because of me, why ARE they in London?

"Are you getting married?" asks Alex bluntly.

Belle giggles. "No, Alex. We're not getting married. This trip is my birthday gift from my parents. They'd bought the train tickets last week thinking I'd want to come down here to visit you, Storm, but, well. . ."

Belle glances at me and my throat tightens, thinking of how angry she must have been with me.

"A trip to London sounded fun anyway. So my parents let me bring Colin instead. They're shopping in Covent Garden now, and we're going to go meet up with them in a couple of hours."

I squeeze Belle and say, "I'm just glad you're here now. And I guess this means I'm totally back on your invite list for Saturday?"

Belle pretends to think about it for a second, then says, "Well, since 1D isn't going to make it, I am going to need a real-life star to perform. . . You know, what with the space theme and all. . ."

I involuntarily scream all over again.

And in that moment, I realize how far I've come since my first brush with fame in Hawaii with Ivy Baxter. I mean, I've gone from performing on Belle's bed with a hairbrush for a mic to performing in front of a packed stadium. And now, after everything that's happened in London, performing for my best friend is the best, most exciting gig in the whole world.

I'm about to explode, I'm so happy. Even with all the mistakes, with all the stress and the tears of the last few weeks, I know that it's all been worth it. Yes, it's been terrible, and I would never want to go through it again, but I've also learned my limits – the things that I *won't* do, the person I won't be. That makes me stronger, more confident and more focused.

Just then, as Tina grills Belle on what she's planning to wear at her own party, I notice that I've been tapping my fingers on the table, drumming out a funky rhythm. An accompanying tune forms in my mind, and I whisper out words to match:

> *. . .I've gotta tell the truth cause these kids they*
> *wanna know,*
> *There's only one Pop Girl, and she's putting on*
> *a show.*
> *Let me hear my Pop Girls, let me hear my Pop*
> *Girls. . .*

I know who I am.

I know my music is good.

And I'm going to share it with the world.

Ready, set, *launch*.